Corridor NINE

SOPHIE STOCKING

thistledown press

Thistledown Press Ltd.
410 2nd Avenue North
Saskatoon, Saskatchewan, S7K 2C3
www.thistledownpress.com

Library and Archives Canada Cataloguing in Publication

Title: Corridor nine / Sophie Stocking.
Names: Stocking, Sophie, 1966- author.
Identifiers: Canadiana (print) 20190137452 | Canadiana (ebook) 20190137460 | ISBN 9781771871815 (softcover) | ISBN 9781771871822 (HTML) | ISBN 9781771871839 (PDF)
Classification: LCC PS8637.T616 C67 2019 | DDC C813/.6—dc23

Cover painting by Sophie Stocking
Cover and book design by Jackie Forrie
Printed and bound in Canada

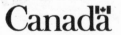

Canada Council   Conseil des Arts
for the Arts   du Canada

SASKATCHEWAN ARTS BOARD | cultivating the arts

Thistledown Press gratefully acknowledges the financial assistance of the Canada Council for the Arts, the Saskatchewan Arts Board, and the Government of Canada for its publishing program.

Corridor NINE

To my family, past and present

BUNE WAITS. THE CLOUD GOWN catches on the calloused tips of his fingers, and moves of its own accord, whispering over the tops of his feet. He's always questioned the uniform, the diaphanous robe in such silly contrast to his gnarled self. Who made these decisions anyhow? He scans the Membrane before him, a screen of light a scant ten feet tall, sandwiched between the smooth green turf on which he stands and the grey ceiling. The Membrane stretches out of his vision on either side, flickering and bellying slightly as if blown from behind by a weak and erratic breeze. It's the ceiling he finds the most oppressive when working on Corridor Nine, it makes flight impossible, and his folded wings itch with the limitation. The Membrane gives the only light.

The Truant could come from anywhere, and Bune melds himself to the limitless stretch of Corridor Nine to feel for some discordant tremor. Then he smells the approach; a pungent mix of coffee, self-pity, diarrhea and despair. He always smells them before he feels them coming in. The disturbance vibrates some fifty fathoms east of him and is penetrating fast. Bune longs to use his wings but the ceiling won't allow it, and for the moment before he musters the energy to shoot himself towards the rupture site, he questions why. Why this tidal pull of dedication that keeps bringing him back to Corridor Nine? This one is a trickster, a riddler, a loophole seeker, and he may remember the terrain, and even Bune himself,

7

from their last go-round. Bune sucks propellant from his endless past, all his memories of horsepower and steam, and fills himself. This way of moving, just blasting one's self to another location is faster than flying but allows no change of course en route. He has the coordinates pinned down as accurately as possible. He sets his focus on the disturbance, gathers himself, and fires.

Fabian

Blackness engulfs him and then he shatters, shards of himself ripping away in all directions. Clinging to his memory of sentient selfhood, he ricochets through space and tries to draw the shards together. The black perforates him. He must make himself whole again. He clenches his memory of teeth, and then unbelievably he begins to coalesce, the shards coming together to form a jagged unfocussed human cloud. Conceit returns first, then more of his traits click into place. His outline fuses. First and most important he has a name, Fabian, and second, he has succeeded in a brilliant escape.

The black now obeys him; it respects his rapidly thickening skin and stays outside the perimeter. His perimeter. He traces it, reinforcing his wholeness. Now he no longer rockets through space but flies slowly. He opens his eyes; he has eyes again and sees more than just black. Far ahead of him a plane of light glows. Fabian rises urgently towards it, like a bubble firing from the murk to explode through the skin of the water. Memory overwhelms him. Hitting that plane of light, over and over, seven times, the impact more painful than a belly flop. He jerks away in terror, flails, and realizes he can slow himself and even move sideways, though the plane of light still pulls him with great certainty. It can't be refused. But then he remembers swimming! He kicks his legs like a frog and shoots sideways. The motion is like those dreams of flying, where you can push off with your toes and decide to go where you like. Fabian laughs for sheer joy and kicks some more, pulls with his arms, and begins to fly in swooping curves, and arabesques. So cleverly, so freely he flies and then he remembers again. Some ominous authority, imprisonment, waits for him behind the light. It will try to catch him as soon as he breaks through and must be avoided at all costs. Fabian picks a direction, although up or down doesn't exist here, only the black and the light barrier. He swims with all his might, trying to get as far from his original trajectory as possible, and watches the barrier closing in on him. Just before impact, a voice in what used to be his head, says distinctly "tuck and roll." Fabian curls his frog self into a ball and ruptures the plane of light with his shoulder.

Bernadette

Bernie drives home and tries to absorb all the connotations to "first day of school". It is the first day of grade one for her last two children, twins Louie and Moira. The older two, Lola and Eben started grade five and eight today, on this too-quiet culmination of thirteen years. Thirteen years of self-erasing, sleep destroying, skin-to-skin frustration, tenderness, boredom, and revelation. She stuck it out all the way, pulled it off, and they are launched now, really quite successfully launched. More had been required of her, to stretch and hold fast, to endure, to consider the other before herself, to delay gratification, more than any other endeavor of her life. Her previous career a shadow in its efforts. So where, thinks Bernie, when she walks out of the school, onto the dusty silence of the sundrenched gravel, swings creaking in the wind, where is the goddamned band?

Bernadette pulls into the driveway, turns off the motor and lets herself into the back door. Angus dances his greeting. The chaos of early morning breakfast and lunch preparation encrusts every counter. The kitchen has assumed the odd gloom of a home vacated; the vapor of her children's being still hangs in the air but has cooled and grown dank. How she loves them, how she misses them, but how gloriously glad she is that they are all finally at school. She is amazed that she can contain both these feelings so fully and at the same time. Bernie walks around the house crying and throwing open windows to let in the air of autumn. It is infused with all she has brought to fruition, but filled as well with the possibilities of things to come. She does not know what to do.

She could take a nap. She never sleeps very well before the first day of school and last night was no exception. She could go to her studio and sort out all the camping gear and old bikes and donate them to the bicycle shop. Turn the studio back into a place where she can work, but to open that long dead possibility seems perilous. How will her postponed battened down ambition erupt? Better to pursue lesser desires for awhile. Maybe she should do some volunteer work. Take up banjo lessons? Buy a gym membership, or get accredited as a yoga instructor? Become a potter as well as a painter or, or, or? Bernie knows she is doing what her friend Marilyn did when her kids went back to school, getting the bends in this sudden vacuum. Louise ended up a chronic volunteer for her children's extracurricular sports and let the rest of her time be cannibalized by the tyranny of the Parent Teacher Association. Breathe, Bernie tells herself, stay calm, go slow. She decides to do the dishes and then clean out the fridge.

Bune and Fabian

Bune arrives at the rupture site in the tornado of his swirling grey self. He stretches his wings out behind him to relieve the cramping, hardly sufficient, and waits. His myriad draperies, scraps, and leaves of cloud that enrobe him, swirl one way around him, then the other. Where is the Truant? He should only have preceded him by a few seconds. Bune jerks as he feels the Membrane rupture somewhere behind him. He whirls around. In the far distance he watches an inverted lesion pierce the Membrane. A bullet of a child jettisons through the orifice. Bune starts to run, he must keep him in sight. The little pink being uncurls as he flies through the grey space, cartwheeling and flailing, fighting against the rotation to regain his feet. Bune runs at top speed, trying to contain himself beneath the tight ceiling and only propel himself forward.

At the same time, Fabian's feet make contact with the mossy turf of Corridor Nine. He rebounds, his immense velocity throws him forward, then he touches down again like an astronaut on the moon. He bounces and stumbles and rolls until finally coming to rest in a small heap. The turf beneath his cheek, pressing against his naked abdomen, his thighs, and chest feels like cool velvet and smells of verdure, every green and leafy thing that ever grew. He inhales deeply and rests.

"Free at last, free at last," he thinks. "I escaped the whole mess, I found the secret door." Bune slows to a walk; now close enough that escape for the Truant is impossible. He watches him acclimatize, staying just back of sight.

The Truant sits up on the turf and looks at himself. He examines his new form; the sturdy little satin skinned body of a boy of three or four. He hugs himself in delight, counts each pink finger and toe; he realizes he feels perfectly warm all over with no need of clothes. He tests the elasticity and strength of his muscles, cackles as he somersaults, then with the control of a gymnast pushes to a handstand. Here he stays looking up at his dangling penis, and then he shouts with joy and does a handspring to his feet. Fabian sticks out his hips and lo, he didn't have to leave it behind! He has all the old equipment, the red and wrinkled overgrown scrotum of a man, with a lolling dangerous inflatable penis to match. He had been rather well endowed in his last incarnation. Yes!

If only, if only . . . his four-year-old paws start patting and feeling his head. Did he get to bring that too? He feels the narrow receding chin, the soft stubble-free skin, and little button nose. Quickly he ascertains the enlarged conical form of his skull. Its overgrown proportions can mean only one thing. His brain! He got to bring the brain! His own brilliant grownup brain! Fabian feels like a child on Christmas morning who could ask for nothing more. He kneels and presses his cheek into the fragrant turf and realizes that he feels no hunger, no satiety, or

12

even memory of food. With a hand he feels between his buttocks for a rectum and to his amazement finds nothing but closed skin, a continuation of the perineum. He lies down on his back and thinks. No digestive system. How wonderful. Free from the unrelenting dictatorship of hunger, the constant feeding, the accumulating shit and constipation, and on the other end of the spectrum the vomiting and diarrhea. His digestive system had caused him untold trouble. His eyes open and he stares around him. The monotone grey space shows no variation in opacity or transparency, nothing to obscure or hide behind, no cloud or drifting fog. The atmosphere waits, completely unvarying in its emptiness. How far does it stretch? Ten feet above the grey ceiling hovers. He wonders what the dull surface is made of. To his left and right the barrier of light continues to either side of him and out of sight. If he turns his back to the light wall, the grey, and the ceiling and velvet turf recede into indeterminable darkness. He hears only static humming and the occasional crackle of the wall.

Fabian feels no hunger and therefore no urgency to search for food. But he still longs for mental stimulation and potential mates. How will he find them? He starts to walk away from the light across the velvet ground, tries to walk in a straight line so that it will be easy to find his way back. He walks and walks towards the dark, but nothing changes, he can find no other barrier or wall, no landmark, certainly no lifeforms. The only difference is an increasing gradient to black. He turns back and is relieved to see the ribbon of light along the horizon. He runs towards it. Here gravity is less strict than his memory of it, and he takes long floating leaps. Because his small

13

body is so coordinated and skillful, he does a series of back flips and somersaults. *How fabulous.* He remembers being in his old body; the struggle and repetition required learning any new skill, and his particular lack of genetic athleticism. He remembers the migraines, bloating and constipation, how bad his knees got by the end, crackling and popping, his blurry vision. This new body offers total freedom, he has only to think of an action and it's as good as done.

He could dance if he wanted, those women he failed to satisfy at various proms and discos should see him now. He conjures up a ballerina in his head and jetés left, jetés right, glissades forward and back, and does a pirouette. Ah, Baryshnikov watch out. Fabian begins to spin in place on one toe. It's not so hard. He spins in a faster and faster vortex and lifts his leg behind him high over his head, arching his back and holding his foot with his hands. He lets the rotations slow, slides forward on one knee and takes a bow, his forehead pressing into the fragrant turf. Silence. No applause, the light wall only whispers and hums.

Fabian remembers his extreme mediocrity as a guard in basketball, his five-foot-eight stature, and how he had never made a team after high school. He wants to show them now, if only he had a hoop and a basketball and a somewhat higher ceiling. He jumps straight up and pretends to dunk, he levitates so quickly he puts his hands up and pushes back against the ceiling to not crack his head. But the ceiling feels like grey rubber and gives way with the impact. He couldn't have hurt himself if he wanted to. "Watch me," Fabian thinks, "watch me now!" He jumps twenty times, vertical leaps to the ceiling. All those fucking six-foot black ball players, beat that! Not even winded, he sits down on the turf. The light wall shifts and glows in silence.

Bune smiles and watches Fabian in his new body. About now, he thinks, the novelty will fade and the reality of Corridor Nine will settle in: the ceiling, the turf, the Membrane to one side, the darkness to the other, and no exit. The horror of this will mitigate the horror of reunion with Bune. He wonders about the pros and cons of some small, nonthreatening noises, or if he should catch him unawares. Perhaps rustling or the noise of a summer wind? Yes, something the Truant would be drawn to, something familiar and friendly. Bune settles on an assortment of birdcalls at a gentle volume, and begins to advance.

Bernadette

Bernie empties the dishwasher and starts to load the dirty dishes from the overflowing sink. Angus hovers hopefully. She puts the kids' plates with remnants of scrambled eggs down on the floor for him to lick off. Angus is the prewash cycle.

"It's just you and me now, bud" she says to him. "You and me for seven hours a day, five days a week." Angus finishes the eggs and sits looking up into her face. Bernie got him from the pound three years ago, after he was rounded up off the Stoney Nation Reserve. Angus looks like the Egyptian jackal god Anubis and is probably a Border collie mix. He smiles up at her now, if a dog could smile, his coyote ears at attention. Glossy and black, his only marking is a white patch on his chest that Lola pointed out looks just like the letter pi. She scratches him behind the ears and he genuflects to downward dog. Bernie obliges, locking his head between her calves she bends over and scratches with both hands up and down his sides. When she's done Angus shakes, glances out the open kitchen door and takes off with a frantic clattering of nails against the linoleum in highspeed pursuit of a squirrel below the bird feeder. This and prewashing dishes are his two greatest passions.

Bernadette turns back to the sink and loads cups and bowls into the dishwasher, scours out the frying pan and the stock pot after transferring last night's Moroccan stew into Tupperware. She scrubs the sink with cleaner until the stainless-steel gleams pristine. For fifteen minutes more, she works on the kitchen, de-cluttering, recycling, throwing out, and wiping counters. Soft air blows in from the doorway. The kitchen is now as calm and immaculate as the sink. She takes a deep breath and relaxes into the odd lack of chaos. Housework feels almost luxurious when done in blissful silence. Next the fridge. Perhaps, though this has never been a pressing ambition, she will become one of those women with a clean fridge.

Bernie opens the fridge and pulls out the produce drawers, behind which salad dressing spilled long ago, and has turned into a leathery adhesive coating. She scrapes this off with a knife, wipes up bread crumbs, desiccated greenery and puddled remains of mouldy fruit, and then starts pulling plastic containers of unknown vintage from the deepest bowels. The unending food and feeding. Twice a week she fills this fridge until she can barely close it, and then in three days her children and husband empty it and complain of nothing to eat. Her head is way under a shelf as she contemplates a bottle of Jerk Seasoning. She thinks she brought it with them when they first moved here six years ago. Why does she keep this stuff? None of her children imbibe Jerk anything. Suddenly, the doorbell rings. Bernie jumps and whacks her head on the shelf, while Angus goes ballistic. Backing out of the fridge, she wipes her hands on her jeans as she walks to the front door. Through the frosted glass she sees the outline of the UPS deliveryman, no doubt bringing some back-to-school clothes she'd ordered for the twins.

"Just a minute" she shouts, "I'll just lock up the dog." Angus can't be trusted with anyone in a uniform, especially the postman. Bernie drags him by the collar and closes him in her bedroom. She goes back and opens the door, but the deliveryman is not in the brown UPS uniform, instead he wears navy. It dawns on her that he is a policeman holding his hat in both hands against his chest. "Oh," she says.

"Excuse me Ma'am. My name is Sergeant Johnson. I am looking for a Bernadette Macomber."

"I am Bernadette Macomber."

"Can I come in, Ma'am? Is there someplace we can sit down?" The kids, Bernie thinks. No the school would have called first. A car accident? But Peter had phoned her when he got to work. "Yes, come into the living room," she says.

He sits down on the couch and Bernie perches opposite him on the ottoman.

"What's happened?"

"I'm sorry to inform you, I have some rather difficult news." Bernie watches his scrubbed face. He is maybe twenty-two, his neck bulging over the top of his too tight collar. A film of sweat shines on his clean-shaven chin and she wishes she could reduce his distress.

"Do you know a Fabian Macomber?" Oh, thinks Bernadette, so this is it. Finally it's come.

"Yes", says Bernie. "Fabian Macomber is my father."

"I am sorry to have to tell you this, but Fabian Macomber passed away sometime last night or early this morning. The cause of death appears to be suicide. He left this note for you." The policeman holds out a legal sized white envelope. Sprawled across it in black Sharpie in her father's messy capitals is her name, and above that are written the words "Please deliver to."

Bernie takes it and pulls out the folded eight by twelve-inch piece of white bond. The same big writing that she has seen so many times. It reads: "Don't feel guilty. I am fatally sick and wouldn't have lasted long anyhow. If there is any money, give it to your kids for college." He hadn't signed it.

Bernie feels electricity buzzing through her body. Cold sweat covers her and only one thought comes to mind; after all these years of hiding from him she must go to him, she must go find her father.

"Where is he?" she says, and then "I have to phone my husband." She walks to the kitchen and picks up the phone, her hand shaking so hard that it is difficult to hit a button and she is grateful that Peter's office number is on speed dial. He answers.

"It's me. There is a policeman here. He came to tell me." She takes a deep breath so she can say the words, "He came to tell me my dad killed himself. I have to go find him now."

"What?" says Peter. "Slow down. A policeman, your dad? Oh my God. Where is he? Where are you going? Find out, and I will meet you there." Bernie turns to the policeman.

"Where is my father?" she says.

"At the Medical Examiner's Office. I'm very sorry but you'll need to come with me for purposes of identification."

"Yes. I'll go." And then to Peter, "the medical examiner's office" and she puts down the phone without disconnecting and tries to think what to do next.

"Just bring your purse Ma'am" says the young man and leads her out of the kitchen.

If this is all there is, thinks Fabian. Would that be all right? He rolls onto his side, propping his big head up on his preschool hand and stares at the light wall. Who would have thought, the place reminds him of a movie theatre with a much nicer carpet. He had been hoping, of course, for billowing meadows and psychedelic sparkling streams, Islam's paradise with its virgin companions, or perhaps Odin's Valhalla. In Valhalla he could have played a great warrior, battling and dismembering all day and then putting the pieces back together and shaking hands with his brothers in arms. In the evening there would be feasting and frolicking with the Valkyries, those Nordic nymphets.

What, after all, had caused his suffering? People! His mother first and foremost, the frustration of beautiful women, and his wife's insistence on children when he so desperately needed all the nurturing for himself. Tall

19

men of course had been a hindrance, they always got the women; black tall men got the women and scored the baskets. But who could blame them given the opportunity; he would have done the same, so that really brought it back to women. Women and mothers were the problem. They had what he needed, but unfortunately his need could never be satisfied, because they were so stingy and withholding.

So here the major frustration of his life was spared him, and he didn't even have to eat. He wasn't cold. Fabian wondered if his "equipment" would functional in this funny place. If so, he could spend his time in self-flagellation alternating with bouts of healthy and acrobatic exercise. He assumed he could still sleep. Look on the bright side, he told himself, all of the crap you got to leave behind: bureaucratic gridlock in every human institution, urban sprawl, environmental devastation in all directions, "superbugs" breeding and cross pollinating in airplanes and hospitals, famines, genocides. Committees, and vegetarianism, and women CEO's click-clacking down the hallways of power in their high-heeled shoes. And ugliness, how it had pained and offended him, beautiful young women covered in tattoos with grommets in their ears. Here there was nothing that was ugly.

Fabian watches the shifting opalescence of the wall. So beautiful, and the sounds the wall made were almost responsive to him, almost conversational. Perhaps he could have a relationship with the wall? Perhaps there was some way to *fuck* it? Fabian stares at the wall, and it gives off a long come-hither hum. He gets to his feet and walks forward.

"Hello wall," he says and then reaches out his hand to touch it. Was it solid or vapor or maybe just electricity? He reaches forward and expects to feel the smooth flexible inside of an abalone shell, he hopes it will be warm, but his hand goes right through up to his armpit and he feels nothing. Fabian pulls his arm back in alarm, remembering the Black on the other side. The wall makes a series of annoying lip-smacking noises. He wants to kick it.

"That's all?" he shouts at the wall. He goes back to his hyperbolic bouncing, and then he sits down, not even breathless. Never getting tired begins to frustrate him. He pats the turf and thinks maybe he could have a relationship with it. He could dig a hole in the fragrant velvety softness and . . . He begins to scrabble at it with his fingernails, is there earth underneath, then jumps back with a yelp. A shard of blue light zigzags out and bites his hand with a fierce electric nip.

If this is all there is, he thinks, *if this is all there is* . . . People had always made him so miserable, how unfair that he could not have left loneliness behind too. He hangs his head between his knees and cries. There are no salty tears though; crying without tears feels as unsatisfying as an interrupted yawn. Fabian yowls and screams and swears for awhile in his impotent little boy voice, then in a pause between expletives he hears a noise. He freezes. Did he imagine that? No, he hears it again clear and sweet, *Chick-a-dee-dee-dee,* and then, *Chick-a-dee-dee-dee,* how poignant that sound. Hiking with Margaret and Bernadette and David. The scent of fir trees floods his memory.

The call is coming from behind; he swivels around and stands up. The light wall stretches away receding to its vanishing point like a perspective exercise he remembers from high school art class. The grey nothingness comes up to meet it and try as he might there is nothing to see, certainly no chickadee flirting and swooping through the grey space. Then he hears a different call. A nagging nasal and insistent *wock, wock, wock a wock, pjur, weer weer,* the sound familiar to him, *wock, wock, wock a wock, pjur, weer weer,* black-and-white magpies fighting over a bone in the snow, suddenly a honking cacophony of Canada geese flying low. Then silence, still he sees nothing. *Chick-dee-dee-dee,* again that sweet trill, and far off in the grey there is movement. He strains his eyes and watches a tiny rain cloud that seems to form and float just above the horizon, and then begins to grow, advancing towards him he realizes at a rapid rate. Again, the wild spring honking of low-flying geese but much louder now, Fabian covers his head and cowers, but quickly uncovers his face to watch the cloud. Perhaps it is a tornado of birds?

The cloud grows and grows, he stares mesmerized, too relieved at the sensory stimulation for fear, but as the bird noises get louder in a bizarre tangle the cloud also grows and takes on detail. He hears the roar of a mighty wind. Torn fragments spin away from the centre of the cloud, scraps of drapery; at the top something protrudes and at the bottom he sees a smaller whirlwind of motion.

"Oh no" says Fabian. "Oh no!" *Wock, wock, wock-a-wock, pjur, weer,weer.* The bump at the top is a head, a terrible head, he remembers now in a visceral way. Running is futile. He curls up in a ball and a cold wind hits him, *Chick a dee dee dee, chick a dee dee dee.* Fabian huddles and shakes. He hunkers before those great feet, his jailor, how could he have forgotten? Then intense annoyance at the trickery overwhelms him.

22

"Turn off the goddamned bird soundtrack!" snaps Fabian.

"Birds of the Rocky Mountain Foothills" says a voice as rooted as a mountain of limestone, yet liquid and surging, a tidal current, the Gulf Stream.

↢⬦↣

Peter stands behind her in the waiting room and puts his warm hand on her shoulder. The only warmth in the room, but she can't stand the sensation. She shrugs away from him. She is as cold inside as this institutional linoleum, as the fluorescent lights. Staying refrigerated seems the safest way.

"I so wish you didn't have to do this," says Peter.

The door with the wired glass window opens and a man in blue scrubs comes through.

"Are you the family of Fabian Macomber?"

"Yes," says Peter, and they follow him down a hallway through chemically sterile air.

They enter a small room with a metal rolling table in the centre. A huddled shape lies under a white sheet with a steel retractable light hovering above. The man folds back the sheet. Peter starts to put his hand on her shoulder again.

"Don't touch me," she snaps and steps forward. She barely recognizes him as the same man, but then she hasn't seen him for seven years. Her father lies curled, his knees folded up and his hands clasped under his chin like a baby in utero. His face peaceful as sleep. Stubble covers the yellowish skin of his receding chin, even more receding now in his old age. He reminds her of some ancient turtle. No longer is his head shaved in sympathy with the Neo Nazi skinheads' fashion he had adopted when she last saw him but has grown out silky and white around his bald crown. How skinny he looks. A diarrheal stench surrounds him, and yes, even now he smells of coffee.

"Sorry about the smell. It's a normal reflex at death. All the sphincters give way. The funeral home will clean him up and lay him out properly once the rigour mortis relaxes. Says the man in blue scrubs. "Is this your father Fabian Macomber?"

"Yes"

A red abraded two-inch strip of skin shows around his neck.

"Why is his neck like that?" asks Bernie.

"We had to remove a plastic bag from his head. He sealed it around his neck with duct tape."

"Why? I don't understand."

"He used helium gas I think they said, with a hose from the canister into the bag."

"Oh," says Bernie. How like her dad. He had always loved tape and adhesives. She remembers the few times he packed her lunch for school. How her sandwich had been entombed in tin foil and bound this way and that with masking tape.

"Daddy?" she says into his quiet face, but she does not want to touch him. Turning away she stumbles into Peter and he wraps her in his arms.

"Let's go now," says Peter and they go out the door and down the hall. Bernie can't feel her feet. Sitting in the car she watches herself as she jerks out violent sobs. When she finishes she wipes her eyes on her sleeve and, looking at Peter, thinks how old he's suddenly grown.

"What do I do now?" asks Bernie.

"I guess we get him cremated. Take care of any belongings. I suppose he left a will."

"That's not what I mean," says Bernie. "I don't know what to do! How do I live with this?"

"With what?"

"I *hurt* him, probably a lot."

Peter starts the car. "Don't go there, Bern. You did what you had to do to stay sane under the circumstances. Don't torture yourself," and Bernie repeats the words all the way home in her head; *what you had to do, what you had to do to stay sane.*

They roll into the driveway. The modernist flat-roofed house that Peter designed for them suddenly looks hollow. Bernie follows Peter up the kitchen steps. He unlocks the door and they both jump a bit when they see Eben standing lanky and awkward at the island. He keeps pushing his overgrown auburn bangs out of his eyes with the back of his wrist as he applies peanut butter to a bagel. Without quite looking up he grunts an incoherent greeting.

"Why are you home so early, Ebe?" asks Peter.

"Early dismiss . . . " mumbles Eben in the cavernous new voice spliced into what used to be their son.

"What?" says Peter, "God how I miss you actually talking to us. Enunciate. I can't understand you."

He looks up at his father and mother, ready to roll his eyes, and says distinctly and patiently, "On Fridays we have early dismissal." From under his bangs he assesses the faces of his parents.

"What's happened?" Eben asks. "Something's happened."

25

Strangely, life continues, even after your father gasses himself with a tank of helium rented from Toys "R" Us. Bernadette carries on doing the things she has always done, but while the rest of the world continues to live in the golden sunlight of early fall, she descends into a grey and steely universe. She must walk through this harsh gravity alone. She doesn't know why she feels so much grief. In the end she decides that their separation in life had been illusory, that the pain she feels resulted from the severing of some invisible cable of kinship.

Daytime means moving resolutely forward through the gritty thickness of time, but at night guilt ambushes her without pity while she lies defenseless in her sleep. Bernie dreams of her father glowering at her from behind tree trunks in a park, a rotund and bearded faun, darting from tree to tree as she tries to feed her children a picnic of plastic food. One night he stands in an upstairs window of her house while she looks up at him from the lawn. He scowls at her, shakes his finger and lectures through the glass as he moves to each of the second story windows, always finding her below with his irate eyes. From this one she wakes up with a shriek, clutching and scrabbling at Peter. But the really dangerous dreams are the ones where he is kind.

Bernie makes sandwiches at seven in the morning but has been awake since three. She needs to buy more mayonnaise and she uses a spatula to scrape out the bottom of the jar, spreads it on eight pieces of bread, and then layers on mustard and ham and spinach. This level of sleep deprivation would normally render her incoherent, but the dreams fire her with anxiety and

26

adrenaline. If only he had never done anything decent, if the craziness had been constant her entire life, but there was an earlier father who built a toy oven from a wooden cupboard with burners lit by red light bulbs, who munificently and extravagantly tossed art supplies on her work table. Perhaps she will never sleep again. She cuts oranges into boats and fits them into the kid's lunch kits. There is no baking, and after digging through the back of the cupboard she finds a fossilized roll of chocolate digestive biscuits. They are running out of groceries. She needs to start functioning again. The kids have been watching hours of movies while she sits on her bed and stares into space or takes long drives in her car listening to Chris Smither cds.

Peter stumbles into the kitchen in his pajamas. He kisses her in passing on his way to the sink to fill up the coffee maker.

"How did you sleep?" he asks.

"Fine for awhile, but I had another dream."

"Why don't you go to the doctor and get some sleeping pills. This is crazy, did you take the Gravol last night?"

"I took it, and it knocked me out but then I woke up. I can't take another one at three in the morning if I'm driving the kids to school."

"You're too tired. It's not safe to be driving at all."

"I know." She changes the subject. "What do I do next, I wonder?"

"I guess you have to figure out what to do with his house."

"I have to go in there and sort it out."

Peter gets a box of cereal out of the cupboard and shakes some into a bowl.

"Why do you always have to do the hard thing, Bernie, and always on your own? Let people *help* you. Hire someone to clean it out. I don't want you retraumatizing yourself. Just get an estate company to go in and sell anything of value, and then we'll list it with a realtor."

Bernie is silent as she fills juice containers. Finally, she says,

"If I go back in there, I can get the evidence I need to stop feeling guilty and finally sleep."

"Evidence you need?"

"Proof of the insanity, of how I had no choice. I need to find the books he wrote at the end."

"That's twisted," says Peter, leaning against the counter, cereal spoon in hand.

"I know, but it's the only way I can get free of this. She closes the insulated lunch bags. "This is sad, but if I can hate him, I'll be safe."

"Alternately, you could just go for counselling. Let's talk with David, he could recommend someone."

"No," says Bernie shaking her head. A powerful sense of direction fills her for the first time since Fabian died. "I think that's the way out, I think that's what I have to do."

"Well, I'll come with you after work."

"You know, I'm just going to go. I'll do it when the kids are at school, there are piano lessons and Lola needs help on her science project tonight. I've got to start being present again, the evenings are for the kids."

"We could get my mother to come on Saturday and watch them. At least take a friend with you, someone." Peter gets the milk from the fridge.

"No. I'm sorry, I need privacy to do this. I don't want to be worried about someone else's reaction to what I'm going through." The dog comes in to say good morning and Bernie leans over and scratches Angus above his tail. "I'll just take Angus. Then I'll be okay."

From upstairs they hear the drumming of Eben's shower. Bernie checks her watch, seven-thirty.

"God I'm late. Could you wake up the twins before you go?" Bernie asks. "I'll get Lola going."

⊸⊝⊸

"Now stop turtling," says the voice, rich in timbre, booming yet quiet. "Sit up, let's have a look at you. See how you've grown.".

Fabian's memory of a digestive track ties itself in knots, flight or fight, his bowels should empty now, but again like the crying, nothing of any substance occurs. He hugs his cherubic knees and in the little boy voice produced by his new set of vocal chords, whimpers "no, no" into the turf. Eventually he finds the courage to raise his head.

"Ghahhh!" he shrieks. The wrinkled muscular talons of a huge bird of prey, the claws black and gleaming, seize and puncture the turf just four feet from where he crouches. Above the legs, overlapping finely wrought feathers of grey rise over the proud barrel chest and lighten to white. The golden eyes of an immense eagle stare at him from below the glowering feathered brow, ear tufts sweep up alert and urgent. Fabian starts crawling backwards on his knees. He realizes the body and back legs of the creature are those of a tawny lion, tensed to spring, the fur terrible in its unearthly softness.

Formidable eagle wings rise out of its back. The great hooked beak opens.

"Come little tadpole. Stop the cringing and moaning. Don't you remember me? Perhaps last time we were together I was in another form. Just wait, how is this?"

Fabian rolls off his knees and onto his feet, his eyes glued to the creature while his body begins to pivot.

"To run would be futile. I am very large, and you are small, now watch. This may be preferable?" A sound of transference and shifting, and in a flurry of wings and fur the creature, Fabian realizes was a living mythical griffin, transforms into a monstrous wolf. Grey and long limbed, he fixes Fabian with the same golden kohl-rimmed eyes. One paw comes forward gingerly, the next one follows.

"The noble and loyal wolf," it intones in that same voice. "The ancestor, the genetic font, the very source of 'Man's Best Friend'. You mustn't fear me. Now reach out and feel my fur. How soft I am. Surely, once you owned a dog?"

"I'm no fool," squeaks Fabian. "My mother read me 'Little Red Riding Hood'. Wolves are crafty and not to be trusted." He persists in his incremental backwards creep.

The wolf sighs and sits down on his haunches. With his back leg he reaches forward and scratches vigorously at a deific flea biting his neck. When he finishes he stares at Fabian again. "You won't give me a pat then?"

Fabian shakes his head and keeps backing up.

"Please stop with the creeping, I will have to go into stalk mode, and you won't like that. Now, try to take a few deep breaths, to calm yourself, and I'll show you the other option. There really are only three." Again, the shredding merging sound, and the wolf melds from his

30

horizontal form upward, the grey fur weaves this way and that until it falls in quiet folds. The feet are those of a man, although calloused and horny as a desert nomad's. Fabian lets his eyes rise through the folds of drapery, like storm clouds. Big, knotted, but blessedly human hands. Up and up, Fabian's eyes skim across a hominid face and then take in the mighty and stereotypical angelic wings. He exhales a deep sigh and sits down. He'd always longed to meet an angel. The face was long and serious; multiple wrinkles v'ing out from between the beetling grey brows. A furrow runs from inside each squinting golden eye to the corners of the somber slit of a mouth. A hooked nose. Grey hair sprouts away from a receding widow's peak. Fabian stares perplexed. The angel's demeanor reminds him of some hard bitten, smoky detective.

The filmy draperies and the wings are the only angelic accoutrements.

Bune plucks at his diaphanous robes. "Standard issue," he says. "You are unknotting. That is good. We should introduce ourselves, I am called Bune, and your name on this, your seventh rupture of the Membrane, would be?"

"F-F-F-Fabian, Fabian Ma-Macomber."

"I see. Oh, I forgot, there is one other option." The angel snaps his fingers. Three heads instead of one now sprout from the shoulders of the being. Fabian screams and somersaults backwards. "You see, I can keep them all facing forward at once, or if you prefer, we can rotate them." He clicks his fingers together again, and with each snap the three heads swivel around the neck, taking their turn at front and centre. "Griffon" croaks the eagle beak, "dog" growls the wolf head, "or man" intones the angel. "Forgive me, this is counterproductive. You have tightened up again. We'll go back to option three. But all of these are necessary, and we will use them at one time or another." Bune snaps his fingers and the two extra heads sink down into his shoulders and disappear. He waits for Fabian to calm down.

"How are you enjoying your new body?" he asks conversationally. "You are not very proportionate, a little heavy on the top and the bottom, and very young in the middle." He takes a few steps back and squats down on his heels, his wings rustle and twitch behind him, and Fabian notices that the tips crimp out sideways where they meet the turf. He wonders if this is uncomfortable.

"It's not an issue," says Bune. "No feeling in the feathers. But they get very twitchy with the lack of exercise in Corridor Nine." From his sitting position he stretches them up and out, leaning into their furthest possible extension. "The only way to get a decent stretch in here is when I'm sitting down!"

Shock and awe at the sight of Bune rubberize Fabian's jaw muscles so that he can only mumble scraps of words.

"Wh-wh-where?" he finally manages to get out, and Bune responds as though he had spoken a whole paragraph.

"Do you not remember anything from your previous ruptures?" Fabian nods.

"When I came in, I remembered hitting the light wall, and I knew someone was waiting to catch me. That's what I remembered. Has it always been you? I mean waiting every time I try to escape the system? You've always been the jailor?" he asks with bitterness.

"Well, no. They assigned me on your fifth rupture. I'm the last resort for acute truancies. But we will proceed more easily if you think of me as your guide, a teacher perhaps. This opportunity lies before us, you see, for the next little while, a holding period if you like, to work through various issues that hampered the success of your previous assignment. Your refusal to actually complete assignments is of course central to your lack of progress."

"What . . . ?"

"Assignments, lifetimes. You've given up so many now. This was your seventh rupture, your seventh suicide. It has become a habit for you, to 'bail out'. One more truancy and you'll no longer have access to Corridor Nine, or to me, of course."

"What happens then?"

"Mulch. You'll be sent down to the mulch pit, where the bonds of self are dissolved, and you become just building material, raw ingredients for other beings. Do you understand therefore, the urgency?" Fabian nods dumbly. His selfhood is more precious to him than anything. He does not want to be "mulched," yet even now so dumb and tongue-tied, in the back of his mind he starts to plot a map. "You are here," it begins, "in Corridor Nine."

"So this isn't all there is," asks Fabian. "If this is the 'ninth' corridor, there are others. Why does it look this way, what shape is it, where does it stop?" He gestures towards the dark that recedes off to his right. Where the hell, he wants to ask, are they hiding Valhalla?

"A donut, it is shaped like a donut, and it encircles all the lifetimes of man. The dark extends for a long way radially all around, until you hit the outer wall. I know you are thinking of an exit, but I must guide you there. It would be impossible to find it on your own. Why don't we walk now? Exercise aids relaxation, and you must become accustomed to me so that we can begin." He rises from his squatting position and Fabian follows suit. His head comes to the angel's hip bone and he remembers walking as a boy, holding his father's index finger in his chubby child hand. But you can't hold the hand of a supernatural being, besides he doesn't want to. Resentment burns quietly in his chest. My jailor he thinks, my "guide." Fabian stifles a snort.

Bune looks down at him from under his protuberant eyebrows. "Ready?" One gnarled foot steps forward, making the cloud gown fold and billow. Fabian extends his own pink paddle-shaped foot, his dimpled leg, and they start. The angel tries to walk at a slow and measured pace, and Fabian trots three steps to his one. Every fourth step he must add a quick skip to catch up. Bune walks closest to the receding dark, with Fabian on the inside near the Membrane. He turns his head and studies the shifting opalescence as they pass.

"What, why, I mean, how come Corridor Nine is like this? No food, or, or, or anything," he finishes lamely.

"Corridor Nine facilitates the conditions most conducive to learning for distractible beings such as yourself. There is no need for food here. In your lifetimes you depended on a symbiotic relationship with bacteria in order to obtain energy and comfort. They fitted you with that myriad looped and twisting bacteria-containing tube, a messy and difficult technology."

Fabian nods his head in agreement. "It was a real pain in the ass," he says. "So, we need no sustenance then, of any kind, when we are here?"

"Sustenance and comfort are still necessary but here they are provided by the ground, this turf we walk on." He stops and has Fabian kneel down. "Breathe in the ether of the turf," instructs Bune. Fabian inhales. He smells fir trees, crushed juniper berries, waves of seed-laden grasses *shooshing* in the wind, bread and apples baking. A smile creeps over his sullen face and deep satisfaction fills him. Sated and replete, for a moment he almost trusts.

"Sleeping on the turf is of course extremely restorative. You've never had as good a sleep as you can get on Corridor Nine. It compensates somewhat for the limitations while I'm here."

Fabian wonders where Bune normally lives, if angels or demons, he wasn't sure which, require mundane things like homes. "So, if this place, Corridor Nine, is a holding place . . . " a sudden thought strikes him, "Corridor Nine is purgatory?"

"I suppose, but that sounds so negative." They were walking again, Fabian doing his four steps and a skip. "Why don't you just extend your stride a bit?" asks the angel. "Small consistent leaps, there we go. You'll find you won't get tired."

"How will walking relax me if I can never get tired. I miss getting tired," grumbles Fabian. "What's the point? And where do you live when you aren't here keeping track of me? I want to see the big picture, the Master Plan," he says flailing his baby arms, "Why are we always kept in the dark? We have to concoct those kooky religious theories on our own. Finally, I'd like some definitive answers!" He scowls up at Bune and stomps his small foot into the ground.

"How quickly you accommodate, tadpole," murmurs Bune. "From terror and awe to entitled indignation in under an hour. Well yes, you will get some answers, that will be one of the lessons, 'Overview of the Master Plan,' but first we'll do one full rotation around Corridor Nine."

"But you said Corridor Nine encircles all the lifetimes of man. We'll never get all the way around!"

"The lifetimes of man are not so extensive, there are only so many essential variations. In Earth terms, circum-navigation is equal to a one-hour moderate jog, I think. Come on, we are already a quarter of the way around."

◦◦◦◦◦

Peter had gotten the twins up and left for work, and Bernie was working as fast as she could to beat the clock through her haze of exhaustion.

"You can't expect me to eat that," says Moira, staring at her fried egg. "You know eggs make me want to throw up."

"For the love of God, we're almost late! Please just for once, eat an egg!" Moira's face crumples into an expression of abject nausea. "Okay then. Louis can you eat an extra egg?"

Louis stares at the computer screen mesmerized by *The Magic School Bus*. He opens his mouth to reply but before he can form a word the impetus dissipates. "Lou! Do you want Moira's egg!" shouts Bernie. No response. She puts the fried egg in front of him and he picks up the fork and begins to shovel it into his mouth.

"So, what can I feed you then Mo?"

"Cheese toast?" asks Moira. Bernie looks at her watch. She has exactly eight minutes to get them all out the door, and the twins haven't brushed their teeth or combed their hair and are sockless.

"Okay, cheese toast, but turn off the computer and go get brushed and find some socks. Louis, turn off the computer!"

"Just a sec," mumbles Louis through the egg. Bernie walks to the computer and reaches behind to hit the power button, as she does so, both twins grab her wrist and try to pull her hand away. "It's almost done, Mom, just wait, just wait. Today is a media day. You *promised*!"

"We have eight minutes to get into the car, does anyone understand that?" She is pulling their grappling and suctioning little fingers off her arm, but Louis starts pushing her backwards while Moira twists her wrist.

"Does anyone understand the issue of fucking time!" yells Bernie. She sweeps away Moira's rolling chair with her leg and gets Louis' interfering arm out of commission by bending it behind his back. With her other hand she can just reach the power button on the back of the screen with the tip of one finger, and *The Magic School Bus* fizzles to black. She wants to kill them. She wants to swear a blue streak for the remaining seven minutes. The twins stare at her with bruised and offended looks on their faces. She takes a deep breath and manages to tamp down the rage.

"Teeth, hair, socks. Go now!" and the twins shuffle down the hallway. "Lola, are you organized, did you pack your books for the science project?" Lola sits dressed, fed and ready in an armchair reading *Tin Tin*, her red-blonde curly hair artistically styled with a diagonal French braid. She looks up. "Yup," she says, "I packed it." Bernie turns on the broiler and sticks a piece of bread under the flame. She walks to the foot of the stair and yells, "Eben, are you ready? Have you eaten anything?" A faint mumble and the scraping of chair legs suggest he hears her. She goes back to the broiler, pulls the now toasted piece of bread out of the oven, scatters grated cheese on the untoasted side and slides it back under the heat. She looks at her watch. They have four minutes. Eben's heavy flat-footed tread comes down the stairs and he stands behind her shoulder now, looking over her head at the remains of the food scattered on the counter.

"Where's my breakfast?" he says. "You fed everyone else didn't you. Why can't you feed me breakfast anymore?"

"Christ, Eben! You're fourteen years old. I told you that you and Lola were in charge of your own breakfasts; I even reminded you when I woke you up. It's not so much to ask, is it?"

"Yeah, Eben," says Lola piously from her armchair. "I made an omelet and I even squeezed my own orange juice. If you weren't always playing video games — "

"Be quiet Lola, this is none of your business," says Bernie

"Yeah, shut your prissy little . . . "

"Eben!" In the nick of time she pulls the slightly scorched cheese bread out of the oven, cuts it in two and puts it into a plastic bowl. She grabs her go-cup go cup of coffee from the counter.

"Well get something to eat quick, grab a power bar and an apple or something. *Coats! Shoes! Backpacks!* Let's go! In the car now!" she bellows down the hall in the direction of the twins. "Where's that damn dog? Angus come!" Angus trots cheerfully down the hall and when Bernie gets out the leash, he starts leaping around kids putting on their shoes and finding backpacks. Finally, she manages to hook him by the collar and clips on the leash, the tangle of them squeezes out the door and she pulls it shut behind them. Standing beside their oxidizing beige minivan she feels in her purse and realizes the keys aren't there.

"God damn! God damn! I locked the keys in the house!" Bernie drops Angus's leash and her go-cup on the lawn. She kicks the minivan in the tire, thumps her fist on the hood, and peers through the dirty window to see if the keys are still in the ignition. Turning around she shouts at her baffled children, "I just want to get in the fucking, goddamned, car!" and then she begins to cry.

They all stare at her; the low morning sun flames their hair into aureoles of light. Angus gyrates anxiously between the children's legs. They look sideways at each other. Lola and Eben step forward and each put an arm around Bernie as she continues to cry.

"Her dad dying from the heart attack, don't you think?" she hears Eben say to Lola over her head, which makes her cry even harder.

"I thought people were sad, when someone dies, but Mom just seems angry all the time," says Lola. They are both rubbing her back. She must pull herself together.

"Go get the spare key from the garage," says Eben to the twins. Blearily she sees the two seven-year-olds run to the padlocked swing gate, but before Moira can manipulate all the numbers of the combination lock Louis has scaled it and jumped down on the other side. He sprints through the backyard, darts into the garage and comes out again waving the key. He vanishes into the back of the house but in a minute appears at the front door smiling and shaking Bernie's big bunch of keys in the air.

"Here you go, Mom," Louis says running up to her "it's okay. Here are your keys. You can get in the fucking car now."

∌∍∌

Bernie sits staring blankly through the windscreen. The children have disappeared into the school fifteen minutes late. How much damage she wonders, had she done? How many times did she yell and swear, and here they were parenting her more than the other way around. What a wreck of a morning. Through her sleep-deprived fog she tells herself that every parent messes up now and then, the vast majority of the time she has been rational and decent. They have a solid foundation, don't they? Little outbursts like this in the long run will create no lasting injury? The important part is to apologize and normalize the whole "incident" for them, and she had done that.

Whole she thinks, her overriding intention for all her children, and remembers the first day after Eben's birth. Baby Eben's head and back lie cradled on her thighs, his newborn feet reposing on her puffy post-delivery stomach. She and Peter and this new pivot point rest in the sunny quiet of their home. The hospital discharged her only an hour and a half ago. Apparently, she is capable of keeping a baby alive or they surely would not have let her take him home. "I just want to get him out whole," she says to Peter, who is leaning over the back of the Ikea armchair watching the baby.

"What do you mean? He looks pretty okay to me, no missing parts."

"No, I mean from his childhood. I want to get him out psychologically intact and undamaged. Do you think that's ever been done? How many people do you know who aren't carrying substantial childhood baggage?"

"Not too many," says Peter.

"Think about my dad for instance, what he might have been like with different parents."

"Well no one's going to have a perfect childhood, and you can't blame your parents for everything. Your dad made his choices."

"I know, but I just wonder if it can be done."

Eben was a spring baby. Bernie watches the poplars in the playground just starting their transition to September yellow, and a woman walks by pushing one of those new whizzy strollers. Bernie turns the key in the ignition, and after some quibbling the minivan starts up. She pulls away from the school, drives down the quiet side street and then turns left onto busier Sixteenth Avenue. Angus needs a walk, but before she does that, she will go see her dad's old house. All she can manage today is a drive-by, but that's a start. Then she'll go home and take a nap. Bernie moves west opposite the downtown-bound morning rush hour, past the strip malls, the college, the stadium. In her rear-view mirror, she sees the black coyote profile of Angus upright and alert. The older, greener subdivisions pass them and then she takes Shaganappi Trail north and turns left onto Crowchild, past more malls and car dealerships. Then she enters the land of monochromatic beige, treeless subdivisions that eat up the countryside. How long, she wonders until the city merges with the little town of Cochrane where she grew up? Finally, she reaches open foothills, now divided into acreages.

Bernie exhales a long breath. Knolls and coulees roll out, their flanks carpeted with golden-leafed aspen, alternating with grassland or sheared fields of grain. The vast sky fills four-fifths of the landscape; clouds pile and rearrange themselves in endless variation against the cerulean blue of fall. On the horizon, the Rocky Mountains beckon to her; beyond them a new land and the possibility of driving and never coming back. Bernie rolls down her window and feels the quiet heat of a fall day, and smells the stubble drying in the fields. The highway curves to the west and then begins its long descent to where Cochrane lies tranquil in the valley. She hears the blast of a CP train as it snakes through the town, its red engine nose keeping company with the curve of the river. Her father is gone. No longer will she fear driving through this town.

In the flat of the valley she turns right, onto the road at the foot of the bluff, cut off from the rest of the town by the highway. Then the final turn onto the last road, Fifth Street. The pavement gives way to gravel, and at the very end, tucked between the toes of the coulee, sits the old house of Cochrane brick, where she grew up. The wheels crunch to a halt and the van sits idling. The house looks out from under the poplars with its peaked dormer face resting in the sun. "What has he done to you?" Bernie wonders. Fifteen years since her mother left. Seven years since she walked out the front door for the last time. The curtains drawn over the windows are the ones her mother sewed and meticulously lined with white sheeting. Suddenly it occurs to her that she doesn't have a key and has no way of getting into the house. She turns off the engine, walks to the back of the minivan, and opens the hatch. She just manages to grab Angus's leash as he leaps towards freedom.

⤝⤝⤞

"Where do we start?" asks Fabian. They are seated, he assumes, back where they began, though there is no way to mark or recognize their location. He wishes he could scratch an X in the turf to mark his spot. "Are we going to go around the circle and tell the group a bit about ourselves and what brought us to Corridor Nine?" he asks.

"It's a very small group," says Bune. "We could just talk if you like, and we can use visuals. The Membrane makes an excellent projection screen. Let's start with something nonthreatening and general . . . "

"I'm not threatened, why would I be threatened?" barks Fabian.

Bune looks at him, his face worn and grained with compassion.

"We'll be looking at your life, how you think it went . . . " begins Bune. Fabian gets up, his outsized testicles dangling between his legs. "How it went? How I think it went?" He paces a circle twice and then begins to bounce very hard, his head almost touching the ceiling. He has to hang onto his balls with one hand. Why have they so overendowed him? With Bune watching he feels silly. After about twenty bounces he calms down and stops, turns to face the demon, his knuckles on his hips.

"Considering the ridiculous nature of the assignment," says Fabian, "I think I did pretty well."

"How so, ridiculous?" asks Bune.

43

"Well my mother first of all. Who assigned me such an inadequate mother?"

"Your Sponsor, you mean? You must have chosen her yourself, following your sixth rupture of the Membrane, although your choices would have been limited, it's true. Now sit down beside me and let's have a look at her." Fabian plants his small bottom on the turf, and sits cross legged, slightly behind the angel. From his vantage point he studies the folds of Bune's gown. He can make out no warp or weft in the fabric and a faint light moves through it. Very slowly he reaches out his hand.

"You can touch it if you are curious," says Bune, and Fabian snatches his hand back.

"I tried to touch the wall and it didn't feel like anything," he says by way of explanation, "and besides, the turf bites. Nothing is reliable here."

"Different rules apply, it's true, and you may not have time to get used to them before you have to go. Look, I think I've found her."

"Found who?" Fabian stares at the Membrane as the opalescence begins to thicken and converge, and he realizes he is watching a moving photo coming into focus.

"Your mother, Evelyn Mary Eddy. Her maiden name, Evelyn Macomber. Here she is just six months old, how adorable . . . " A warm wind, smelling of clover, blows through an open kitchen window. Sitting belly-deep in a porcelain sink in front of the window, a baby with wrinkles like bracelets around her fat wrists coos and hoots and chews on a washcloth to ease her itchy, teething gums. Two graceful and solicitous hands cup water over Evelyn's shoulders, trickle it down her spine so that she tips her head back and gurgles a laugh.

44

"Those are my grandmother's hands?"

"Yes, Bernadette Mary Eddy." The hand holds a small comb and runs it carefully through the platinum wisps of the baby's hair, combing them up to the top of her head and twisting them into a kewpie doll curl. "Do you remember her?"

"Yes," says Fabian. "I wish she could have lived with us, she was so kind. Look how she touches her, my mother never . . . " The hand reaches under a chubby leg and pulls a rubber stopper out of the drain by its silver-beaded chain. "I hate babies," says Fabian. "I don't like to look at them," and he turns his back to the Membrane. The picture flickers on behind him, the baby is lifted out and wrapped in a worn, but clean, towel.

"That part's over. Turn around, watch now," says Bune. Evelyn nestles against the ample breasts that would one day droop to the belt of Fabian's grandma Bernie. The baby reaches out and wraps her paw around a gold locket that lies in the indent between her mother's collarbones, mangles it into her drooling mouth. "No, Evie don't eat that. Where's daddy got to?" Late evening sun washes them as she rocks and jiggles the baby gnawing on her necklace, and stares out the window down the road.

"He was a drinker and a charmer. Mama hated him."

"Well now you know where you got it from. The addictive element, if not the charm." Bune chuckles, "I'm teasing. You had the same black humour and reprobate lure that good girls find so irresistible. At least for a time."

"I wouldn't know. I never met him. Show me more pictures." Bune rubs his hands together, and the mother and child dissolve. Flickering light and shadow emerge, a grove of aspen surrounds a lawn. Women in

45

white calf-length dresses, hair curling and coiling into naped buns, tendrils escaping around their laughing faces. Young men dressed in rusty black suits, some with pomade-slicked hair, assist and interfere in the ladies' game of croquet. The focus moves across the roughly shorn grass to a picnic table full of revelers.

"There he is," says Bune. "There's Harold. The man at the end of the table opposite the young blonde."

Fabian watches fascinated, the young man leans forward across the table, both hands encircling his stubby glass. The blonde blushes and glances down under the intensity of his gaze, and Fabian exults. "Grandpa was a smooth operator all right, look he's working her, he's working her!" Harold turns and looks towards them, tilts his head disdainfully in the shade of his hat. His eyes don't condescend to smile. "My God, he looks like a prohibition Bob Dylan," says Fabian.

⬦⬦⬦

Lola lies in bed reading *Swiss Family Robinson*. Her hedgehog, Cynthia, digs and snuffles, and the impassioned rooting distracts her from her book. She gets up and walks to the cage.

"Are you hungry?" Lola opens the tub of hedgehog chow, and tips some into the food dish. Her hedgehog, Cynthia keeps rooting. "Here, eat your kibble," Lola slides her hand under the furry belly and lifts her over to the food dish, but the wet snout recoils. "Okay, okay," Lola walks naked through the dark house to the kitchen. She opens the fridge door and sees herself reflected in the kitchen window, that new conical swelling under each nipple, and she squats down out of view. From the cheese drawer she takes out three of the waxy squirming mealworms, shuffles backwards, shuts the fridge, and returns down the hall. Passing the French doors, she sees flames glowing and sparking in the portable fire pit on the deck. Her mother stands in the light holding a white piece of paper before her, as if reading to an audience. Lola pauses, then returns to Cynthia's cage and scatters the worms in the wood chips. Cold now, she pulls her pajamas out from the pile of laundry on the floor and puts them on. When she returns to the back doors her father stands looking into the dark. He puts his arm around her shoulders.

"Why aren't you asleep? It's ten-thirty."

"What's Mom doing?" Outside Bernie kneels in front of the fire, folds the white sheet into a paper airplane, and lights the tip in the flame. It catches, and she lays it in the hottest part of the fire, watches it burst, ducks her head as if in prayer. Peter sighs.

"They cremated her dad today. I imagine she's praying for him. She's worried he won't be able to reincarnate or something, because he . . . I mean, you know your mom. Something to do with her Hindu stuff. Now go to bed, buddy. School tomorrow." He kisses her on the top of her head and directs her towards her bedroom by her shoulders.

"Well, what do you believe in Daddy?"

"Mmmm, I don't know. I think we're all energy, and when we die, we maybe join a big energy blanket that surrounds the planet. Our bodies compost, maybe our energy composts?"

"Well, that's pretty weird too, you know. I think reincarnation makes sense. I hope to come back as a snow leopard, or maybe a horse." Peter tucks her into bed.

"How do you sleep with that hedgehog making so much noise?"

"I'm used to her. It helps me sleep actually."

"Good night, then."

"'Night Daddy."

Bits of grit dig into Bernie's knees. She closes her eyes and watches the red glow inside her lids. Receive him, she thinks. His angels, his keepers, please catch him, bring him to where he's safe and can grow. Let him know I do love him. I am sorry I hurt you. Forgive me. Go in peace and start again. Please, please, catch him.

I'll just walk around the house, Bernie thinks. The long grass lies dry and matted and the poplar leaves she used to watch from her bedroom window murmur above her. She imagines they are trying to give her courage. "Keep me safe, keep me safe," the mantra starts, the words that had rolled with her down the highway to see him, until she couldn't visit anymore. Bernie walks along the gravel path that splits at the front door. She goes left, past the south wall where she and David stacked firewood each fall, the space empty now. The two small basement windows are encrusted with dust. In the window wells leaves collect where she hid in games of hide and seek, where once a vole took a wrong turn and tunnelled into that dead end. David picked it up by the stubby tail, showed her the white underbelly and disgruntled rodent face before he let it zip into the grass.

She remembered their phone call the night after she'd identified the body.

Hey, Bern, how's it going?

I don't know how to say this, are you at home? You're not driving, are you? *I just pulled into the driveway. What's wrong?* I have to tell you something hard. I don't know how to start. A policeman came today. Daddy, um, Daddy finally did it. He offed himself. Sometime last night. *What?? How?* Helium, they said, and a garbage bag. I waited until you'd be done work. Where's Louise? Will she be home soon? *How? Helium?* I guess it's a painless way to go, he hooked up a hose to a tank of helium and fed it into a garbage bag he taped around his neck. *Oh my God.* I think it must have been painless. He looked peaceful at any rate. Peter and I went to the morgue and we saw him. *I don't know what to say, wow I, boy.* Yeah, I know, what is there to say? Do you think you could come? *I don't know, it's a bad time right now with work Bern, I doubt it. Son of a bitch never wasted much effort on me. I have to think.* I'm sorry. *Are you, all right?* I don't know. I'd be all right if I could stop thinking I caused this, you know? That if I'd stayed in touch . . . *He was too crazy for human consumption Bern, he had a gun collection, remember? You were worried about your kids.* I know. Why can't I make that stick in my brain? The guilt always wins.

Bernie stares into the basement window well and wishes David lived in Calgary instead of Toronto. He won't fly out she knows, a silent agreement on both their parts. Bernie was Fabian's favourite and she carries her father's guilt as her own without question. She must protect David from further harm. She walks around the corner, and pauses, her hand on the sun-warmed brick. At the back of the house facing west they had tacked on a deck. Above it, the four-ply beam that supports her old bedroom balances on three skinny steel poles, their weight transferred into concrete Sonotube pilings — an ugly addition to an historic old home. The Adirondack chairs sit sun bleached and rickety now, one tipped on its side. He never got rid of the half whiskey barrels filled with dirt that her mother had planted with tomatoes and marigolds every summer. Someone has been digging in them, knocking dirt onto the deck. Maybe squirrels, she thinks. Bernie wraps Angus's leash twice around her hand in case one should show up suddenly. She arrives now at the stairs to the deck; on one side is the collection of rocks she brought home from trips and hikes as a child. Among the stones they hid a spare key in one of those plastic imitation rocks with a secret compartment inside. She pokes around with her toe, thinking it couldn't possibly still be there, but then she sees it through the open risers of the stairs, flipped over to reveal the rusty metal cover underneath. She kneels on the first step, and with her other arm reaches through and pulls it out. It rattles. Sliding out the metal cover, with her thumb she sees the old blue key laying there, just a little tarnished. How many times had she let herself in with that key after a day at school? Which would be worse, Bernie wonders, driving home now and not knowing, or knowing and then wondering what to do next.

"Come on," she says to Angus and walks up the steps. The key fits into the deadbolt and with some fiddling turns stiffly. The door releases inward a crack and she pushes it the rest of the way with her foot. Smells hit her. First cat shit, then incense, and last the odd musky smell that her father had always given off. Sunshine spills in through the venetian blind that hangs askew over the sink, slats in disarray. The counters are covered with dirty dishes. Dry cat food and spilled coffee, kitty litter, and cereal encrust the linoleum. Angus twists and hops around on his leash pulling her arm almost out of its socket as he hoovers up the cat food, dragging her into the house to find the actual cat.

"The cat's long gone Angus." The neighbour had apparently taken him in. Mrs. Gotslieg. She must be seventy now. She was the one who had found him that morning, the door blown open by the wind and his cat mewling at her kitchen window. Bernie feels she should go talk to her, apologize, like one would for a dog that barked all day because you left him out when you went to work, or for the leaves that blew onto the neighbour's lawn because you were tardy with the raking.

She and Angus walk across the crusty floor and into the dark living room. The sun dimly illuminates the paisley through the mustard drapes. Her mother's hippie curtains. She walks to the window and pulls them open, dead wasps and flies litter the window ledge but now, at least, the sun fills the room. She turns and faces the detritus of his life. Coffee cups and glasses everywhere, piles of clothes, blankets on the couch, a big screen TV. When had he bought that, she wonders. A Japanese painted scroll of cranes flying over mountains hangs askew. In the corner sits a needleless Christmas tree, each branch encrusted with dusty glass ornaments, some cheap Zellers specials but most beautiful and ornate.

The floor puzzles her, so soft under her feet and then she realizes he has layered cheap oriental carpets all over the living room, in some places five or six thick. Her father's preferred alternative to vacuuming.

She looks briefly in the other rooms but doesn't go into the study where Mrs. Gotslieg found him. She shuts the door to close in the stink of the diarrhea in the carpet. His bedroom is piled with laundry, the bathroom sink spackled thickly with toothpaste. Empty shampoo bottles and old tubes of ointment litter the floor. In every room she finds empty plastic prescription bottles, beside the couch, the bedside table, by the kitchen sink. The few she reads prescribe Percocet or Oxycontin, but some of them are for Tylenol 3s, what he used to take when she was a teenager. Percocet and Oxycontin, she will look them up when she gets home. Angus' furry black side warms her leg, and she hasn't loosened her grip on his leash since they came in. Peter was right. She would go home and get a dumpster delivered to the driveway and find a company that could clean out a place like this.

"Come on, let's go," she says to Angus. They walk out the kitchen door again. She locks it with the blue key, puts the key back in the plastic rock, and wedges the plastic rock into her childhood rock collection. They drive away, but part way up the highway the contorted knot of her stomach refuses to hold her breakfast any longer. She pulls over, crawls across the passenger seat and vomits out the door.

"Will we have to do this in punishing chronological order?" asks Fabian. Bune sits entranced by the flickering images.

"This part is so heartbreaking. The Christmas Harold didn't come home, left for a walk after breakfast and didn't get back until eleven o'clock that night. They had the turkey alone, Bernadette's mother and father (your great-grandma and -grandpa Elizabeth and Herbert), Bernadette, and eight-year-old Evelyn. A Christmas to remember, don't you think, so embarrassing. You can see how that coloured . . . " Bune looks sideways at Fabian who spins on his bottom, rolls his eyes and looks off into the dark. "How that coloured her feelings about men? This is too methodical? What would you prefer?"

"I've heard that story a hundred times. I thought you were going to give me an overview of the 'Big Picture' first. You said you'd tell me after our walk."

Bune stretches his wings behind him, flexing them spasmodically at their furthest extension. They brush in a muscular way against Fabian, toppling him sideways; they feel stronger, more softly napped, than feathers should. Looking closely, Fabian sees they are constructed like leaves, lacking the delicate inter-hooking barbules of an avian feather.

"Hey!" says Fabian. Bune pretends not to notice, flexing his wings back some more and out to the sides, pushing and nudging at the homunculus boy like a dog would a pup. Fabian refuses to relent, rolls away and gets to his feet. "You promised! You said I could see an overview." Hands on hips, he stretches as tall as he is able.

Bune gets up and shakes out his legs, the cloud gown crackles and gives off soft echoes of thunder. "All right, there's no harm in getting a lay of the land. Here, I will put up a diagram of how we are going to proceed over the next while, the course outline, and then a diagram of, how can I express this? I guess you said it best, 'The Big Picture'."

"Yes, a map. Can't we start with the map?"

Bune looks down at him; his rocky face shifts to amusement.

"If you like. Now watch." He gestures towards the Membrane and Fabian's eyes search, frantic and hungry, but then grow puzzled.

"Well it just looks like a bull's eye. You're telling me the Master Plan is some sort of dart board?"

"Let me orient you," says Bune. "The very outermost layer, the darkest stripe is Corridor Ten, the realm of reorganization, this is where the basic building blocks for beings come from. If you fail in your next assignment this is where you'll end up. Like I said before, the bonds of self dissolve, and a mulching process occurs, kind of like composting. Beyond all the time and effort, you've put in I suppose it isn't such a waste because your essence will be reconfigured for some other being."

"Does that hurt?" Bune looks away.

"It's not something you can remember, but definitely Corridor Ten echoes with groaning and gnashing sounds, very noisy. Luckily, I've never been employed there. But let's move on. Here we are thankfully in Corridor Nine." Fabian stares at the second ring, which glows a dark burgundy. A band of light separates it from the third ring, of a less clotted red, and so on. The rings progress towards the centre of the donut. The smallest innermost ring shines a clear pale gold. At the very centre, inky

54

black and spinning, Fabian sees an exquisite planet. It radiates a quivering light so that he can only indistinctly make out the geography. All the rings are separated by an outline of radiating light.

"What are those lines of light," asks Fabian, "between the Corridors? I'm surprised really, this map seems so reductionist, I thought the universe was about expansion."

"Oh, you can find your universe, tucked into the layers of light roughly between Corridors Nine through Six." Bune points toward the Membrane, his craggy finger tracing each of the radiant borders, making them glow more brightly. "Within these bands you see, are housed your assignments or lifetimes. You enter them; I'll have to zoom in, via the Sponsor Ring. Here, do you see?" A circular cut out of Corridor Nine projects forward in greater and greater detail until Fabian can see an outer tracing of pink around the ring of light. "The pink band, the Gateway, gives you entrance into your next assignment."

"What would motivate me to keep moving towards the centre of this bull's eye? It seems like a lot of effort, my last assignment was so horrific, punishing really. Do they get better as they progress? I feel so constricted." Bune reaches out to lay a consoling hand on Fabian's shoulder, but Fabian moves away, hunkering on his heels and gripping his head in his hands.

"Each layer is less and less constricting, with greater freedoms, greater joys, until you reach the centre and that truly is, how do you say it? 'Mind blowing,'" chuckles Bune.

"That's where they've hidden it then?" says Fabian, standing up. He begins to vibrate with excitement, "that's where they've hidden Valhalla!"

"Val who?"

"Valhalla! Paradise! Heaven! The Promised Land!" Fabian hops from foot to foot. Bune clasps his hands behind his back and waits, staring into the middle distance. In a minute Fabian whirls towards him.

"There's got to be a Fast Track plan, shortcuts, points for good behaviour. Something!"

"Tadpole," says Bune, "we must start with patience, step by step, endurance, stoicism. One of your three lessons. Although any corridor can be accessed from any gateway, skipping a level is almost unheard of. It would depend on your intent and the evolutionary level of your Sponsor, none the less very unlikely. You'd need to be a quick study and made of pure material."

"Like skipping a grade in school!" exults Fabian. "My mother had the principal move me ahead in Grade Two . . . Okay, now where is the entrance to this 'Gateway'? What did you call it, the Sponsor Ring? Bune smiles and gestures magnanimously towards the Membrane. A dotted moving light can be seen extending at a right angle from the burgundy band of Corridor Nine into the pink Sponsor Ring.

"Just like the strip of emergency lighting in an airplane," says Fabian. "But where does the entrance lie relative to me, I mean to our position?" Bune zooms the diagram out again.

"I believe this is what you are looking for . . . " a red X appears at the three o'clock position on the burgundy ring, "and the exit is anywhere along the furthest

56

external edge of Corridor Nine, you see the little light?"
Fabian stares at a capricious sparkle that skips and zips,
reappearing unpredictably around the perimeter.

"If it won't stay still, how can we enter through it?"

"You need me. I must take you," says Bune.

Bernie wakes tangled in the blanket on her bed. The
alarm blares. What planet was she on? She flails until
she makes contact with the alarm clock and turns it off.
Two-thirty, but what those numbers signify she doesn't
know. She lies there for five minutes staring at the
moving branches outside her window before it dawns on
her that two-thirty means time to pick the kids up from
school; she has to go in ten minutes to be there by three-
fifteen. Bernie gets up and splashes water on her face.
She brushes her teeth and wishes she had time to wash
her hair. Tonight, she must fit in a shower. She clamps a
cap onto her head and finds a clean sweater.

Waiting in the playground she makes small talk with
other parents. Yes, the weather has been amazing, can't
complain. Are you volunteering for the Science Centre
field trip? Ilene tries to motivate her to spearhead the
next bottle drive. Bernadette wonders how she looks from
the outside, how they possibly couldn't know. All these
people and their normal healthy lives. How was your
summer, I never got the chance to ask? Just dandy. She
couldn't tell them anything, couldn't ask casually, "Does
anybody know of a reliable post-death-cleanup service?"

Finally, the bell rings and the kids start streaming out
of the blue door. Lola comes out first, talking intently to
her friend Gretchen, no doubt about their hedgehogs.

They had been planning on getting their pets together for a social visit on the weekend. Bernie hopes they are right about both owning females. Now the twins. They pick her out of the crowd and run at her, nearly knocking her over with the impact of their daddy-long-leg bodies. Mommy! With the offer of ice cream, they forego the playground and head for the minivan. She follows them, bright globules of light in Bernie's dark world.

"Mom, can we stop at the pet store and get some more meal worms? Cynthia hasn't had a chance to hunt all week."

"Really, do we have to get live ones? It's just the way they squirm, Lola. Couldn't we buy the freeze-dried ones, then I wouldn't have to keep them in the cheese drawer."

"It keeps her sharp, Mom, I think actually she's a little depressed. Insectivores *need* to stalk their prey, it's an *instinct*, like migrating."

Bernie laughs, "Okay, the pet store then ice cream."

"Oh, and Mom, please please *please*, can we stop at Staples? I've run out of elastic bands," begs Louie.

"Your elastic band ball is huge Louie. Will an elastic even fit now? Last time we measured it was ten inches across."

"I'm taking it to school next week for show and tell, please mom."

"Okay, pet store, Staples, ice cream." Feeling wildly benevolent, "anything for Moira?" looking into the rear-view mirror where her skinny girl sits, her head partially out the open window singing one of her stream-of-consciousness ditties. The slipstream partially fills and flaps her cheeks. "Moira, do you need anything on the way home? What's she singing, Louie?"

"Something about 'I don't care, you can't make *me*, you guys can all go climb a *tree*, usual stuff," says Louie.

"Ah yes," says Bernie. She lets everything in the van warm her up. Her three-hour nap has restored her to a level of sleep deprivation that felt like the buzz after two glasses of wine. The sun pours over them. Stepping into Staples, she breathes in the wonderful stationary store smell, reams and reams of paper, erasers by the box-full, paper clips, Duo tangs, those sticky circular hole reinforcers. She loves all of it with a sudden ferocity, so normal, so grounding, the staff people who smile at her and wish her a good night, despite their day marinated in top forty tunes and fluorescent lighting. The girl at the drive-through ice cream window, a tattoo in her cleavage and a stud in her tongue, winks when Bernie thanks her for the lavish doling out of ice cream. She probably lives in a basement suite with her abusive boyfriend and yet she was so kind.

When all the errands are done, they drive home. Walking into the front hall, she sees Eben's shoes and backpack splayed across the floor, proof of his existence and return home on the school bus.

"Eben!" she shouts up the stairs. "Eben, how was your day?" No reply. I yell too much, she thinks, and starts climbing. Forgetting he lives here is becoming too easy. Upstairs she walks noisily to warn him of her coming and then knocks on his door.

"Eben?" he lays on his bed with the duvet pulled over his head, his back towards her.

"What?" he pulls the blanket back and rotates to look at her, pained boredom on his pale and acne-tortured face. He pulls his earbuds out by their wires.

"I just wanted to see you. How was your day? Is there anything on tonight? I was thinking . . . "

"Mom, it was all normal, just a normal day."

"The kids and I saw this cool bike repair place on the way home from school, down by Totem. I guess they help you fix your bike, and it's a great place to go get volunteer experience. Why don't . . . "

"Mom, please, just *go* away. I'm tired." He rolls over and pulls up the quilt. Bernie stands there staring at the long burial mound of her child. She wants to wrestle with him, make him laugh like when he was twelve, wants to give him a back rub, as she always had. The last time happened about a year ago when he'd slept through his alarm. "Don't touch me!" he'd snapped. For awhile she'd asked permission and sometimes, he'd say yes, but at this point it wasn't respectful to even attempt. Bernie turns around and leaves the room.

The twins are outside jumping on the trampoline, shouting and laughing. Bernie walks to Lola's room where a sign is posted on her door, "Hedgehog at Large". She slips in quickly and closes it. They have to be careful in light of Angus's questionable loyalty to Cynthia. Lola lies on the floor on her belly. Beside her, arranged in a labyrinth of wrinkles, her fleece baby blanket twitches and vibrates.

"Watch this Mom! Watch! I've hidden five mealworms; let's see how long it takes her to find them. She's so fast with her nose . . . "

At least she has Lola for another couple years, and a long, long time with the twins she thinks, as she walks into the kitchen to start supper. Tonight, she will actually cook and not just heat up pizzas or order Vietnamese. She must start functioning again, but digging through the fridge and freezer she realizes the scarcity of anything verging on edible. She manages to find two bags of frozen beef raviolis, a large onion that has started to rot at the crown but is otherwise sound, four slightly wrinkled tomatoes, some shrivelled but not decomposing garlic.

Bernie heads to the garden with a knife. She pauses before her studio, the large shed Peter had renovated. He'd insulated it, installed a Franklin stove, and a north facing many-paned window, rescued from some old house. At the peak of the roof perches the sundial her father made from her drawing when she was ten. She'd drawn a long arrow that blossomed at the tail with a sun and a crescent moon. It rotates with a squawk, and she imagines the marble inside the pipe, the pivot point, shattered long ago.

She walks on, climbs the cast-concrete stairs that meander through the modernist garden of tiered beds that Peter designed for her. She had worked on this garden all summer, and the raised beds spill over now with an explosion of growth. First, she pulls carrots, then digs a few leeks, silky and as thick as her thumb, cuts some oregano and flat-leaf parsley, and finds a small zucchini that hasn't exploded to whale-like proportions like the others. She shouts to the twins on the trampoline.

"Lou and Mo come see your zucchini. They've gone crazy!"

In the bed against the retaining wall, cherry tomatoes grow, their laden branches propped up in wire cages. Bernie gathers handfuls of round red and yellow pear-shaped ones, carrying them to the house using the front of her t-shirt like an apron. In the kitchen she washes the dirt off the leeks, chops garlic and zucchini, throws in the tomatoes, and gets it all sautéing in olive oil. She fills the big pot with water and adds a handful of salt. She tastes it. Pasta water should be as salty as the Dead Sea. When the vegetables are soft she mashes them with her potato masher, and seasons them. The ravioli are al dente. Peter and his team are working late on the development permit for his airport project. Terminal D, hopefully ready to proceed to construction in the spring. He won't be home until late. She calls the kids to the table feeling victorious, the clock says six thirty, and the meal actually contains both protein and fresh vegetables. They all sit around the table, except for Eben who deigns to sit on the couch.

"Eben, before you vanish, you have to unload the dishwasher. Then Lola, you load, and Lou and Mo," she looks around, but they are in their room. She hears the rustling, tinkling sound of their hands searching and pushing through piles of Lego. Ah, never mind, she'll scrub out the two pots herself. Eben without any complaint or resistance goes to the dishwasher and gets to work, and when he finishes Lola steps in and fills it with unaccustomed efficiency. Their goodness puzzles her.

Sitting on Lola's bed, Bernie reads *Harriet the Spy* to the three younger ones. Bernie finishes the cliff-hanging chapter, where Harriet's friends find her perfidious notebook, and she must face them for the first time at school.

Bernie looks up and Lola, Louis, and Moira are staring at her transfixed, like dogs waiting to be thrown a steak. Now comes the begging and wrestling match she thinks, as she shuts the book, "*Please* just one more chapter!" but

Lola makes an odd clicking noise with her tongue on the roof of her mouth.

"Remember, guys?" she says to the twins, and then all three of them get up and shuffle off to brush their teeth.

What's up with that, wonders Bernie.

Later she walks around the house switching off lights and turning down thermostat. She checks on the twins. They sleep together in the bottom bunk, Mo's arm thrown over Louis, whose head lolls close to the edge of the bed. Bernie shifts Moira further in towards the wall and then moves Lou. No danger of waking them, they sleep like the dead. The horrible morning and trip to the old house seem a week ago, so different from the calm at the end of the day. Perhaps finally going into the house was the trigger, no more procrastination and worry about the unknown. Maybe that will be enough to keep her asleep tonight. Bernie gets out of her clothes and puts on her bathrobe. She brushes her teeth and, taking her laptop, crawls into bed.

What would the appropriate term be? Bernie types in "after-death disposal" and a list of coroner's offices and funeral homes comes up. No, she had no actual body to worry about. "Cleaning services", but she couldn't ask some lady from Molly Maid to rip out a shit-encrusted carpet. Finally, she tries "suicide clean up" and finds page after page about "biohazard remediation". There are pictures of large friendly men in protective hazmat suits, fabric booties, and respirators. On an American website for a company called Biocare she reads: "Suicide clean up attempts are best handled by our trained professionals. It is recommended that friends and family members, do not try to clean the scene of a suicide for safety and emotional well-being. Contact us!" How wonderful is that, thinks Bernie. She types in "suicide clean up Calgary". Two listings come up on YellowPages.ca.

Bio Trauma Clean up reads the first entry. "We service all of central and southern Alberta, crime and death scene cleaning and remediation, sewage clean up, large scale animal biohazard our specialty." Their office is in Edmonton. It's just one nasty carpet, thinks Bernie, maybe I don't need such a big company. She tries the second listing. "A.D.D.", she reads, "After Death Detail, professional, experienced and discreet. Our family-based business has been serving Calgary since 1982. Let our caring professionals ease your mind during this traumatic time. Estate clean up and disposal also available." That's perfect thinks Bernie, she grabs a pen and the only piece of paper beside the bed, a word search that Mo had been working on, flips it over and writes down the phone number. She closes her laptop, switches off the light and almost immediately falls asleep.

⊶⊷⊶

"Okay, I think we've covered enough for one day, don't you?"

"Has it been a day?" asks Fabian. The Membrane doesn't falter in its opalescing, the grey space behind them continues to recede into black.

"I bet you'll like this. From now on I'll put up sunrise and sunset indicators. We've covered the orientation phase, so a sense of passing time will be helpful, but we've missed sunset. Earth time is about 9:30. You should lie down now on the turf. Breathe in the ether. What does it offer tonight?"

Fabian lies down sullen but dutiful, settles himself into the turf, which softens like a mattress and forms under his hip and shoulder. He breathes quietly for awhile. Roast chicken this time, with crackly salty skin, a symphony of root vegetables. Apricots in kirsch.

"Not bad!" says Fabian looking up at the angel.

"All right now, watch. I'll do a fast-forward until we catch up."

Fabian gazes at the Membrane as it moves rapidly through a stereotypical sunset progression; golden light fades to green, fades to teal, fades to a plushy navy blue. Finally, black and twinkling stars. How annoying, the twinkles are arranged in a grid pattern.

"Couldn't the stars be more . . . ?"

"Ah yes, Northern hemisphere, I forgot." The stars rearrange themselves. Fabian can make out the Big Dipper and Orion's Belt. He feels very sleepy.

"Good night then."

"Night," murmurs Fabian.

Fabian wakes with a jerk and a shot of adrenaline, like he used to after coming down from a high, like a child on the first morning of camp. He remembers where he is, his eyes fly open and he looks around. His heart and stomach grip. Bune is nowhere to be seen. He has left Fabian alone with only this sleeping wolf lying two metres away, nose tucked under tail. Fabian should be sweating. He needs to do something, to eject or leak, but he certainly doesn't want to shout. "I'll just get the fuck out of here," he thinks, and starts crawling backwards. After a reasonable distance he gets to his feet and runs, but in the first strides into the dark he wakes up another degree and feels foolish. Be sensible. It's only Bune. It's only your demon/angel. Fabian snorts aloud and the noise wakes the sleeping wolf.

"Hey!" The wolf sits up and scratches behind his ear, looking around blearily. "Now where has the little tadpole got too?" He peers into the dark and finds the brighter patch; the first golden light of the sunrise indicator, which bounces rosily off Fabian's body. Bune licks his front forepaw, and then gets an excruciating itch between two toes. He goes at it vigorously, his lips pulled back and his teeth scissor as precisely as possible. He finds the flea and feels it pop between his incisors. Angel fleas. He gives himself a shake.

"Little Tadpole," he calls into the gloom, "come back. You know it's only me. Today you need to get over it and give me a pat. Then I'll change back if you want." Fabian stands motionless.

"When you were a boy you had a dog. What was his name? Ah yes, Brownie." Fabian breathes in and starts walking back dragging his feet. He wishes he had pockets to jam his hands into. He stops before the wolf.

"Could you not do that?" he grumbles. "Switch like that without warning. First thing in the morning too."

"I'm sorry, I enjoy the variety. Full angel format gets cramping on Corridor Nine. But just come pat me and then you should have breakfast."

Fabian stretches his arm out, holds the back of his hand under the wolf's nose. Bune sniffs and woofs a laugh.

"You still smell like coffee but not so desperate. Now scratch me behind the ears." The fur of the ruff springs under Fabian's fingers, each hair an infinitesimal jet of energy. He digs his fingers deeper, finding the cool resilience of the skin, scratches under the ear, down below the chin. Bune leans into him, half closes an eye, and grunts appreciation.

"With Brownie, I used to go like this." Fabian, reaches way over, scratches the lower back just in front of the tail. Bune can't help himself and genuflects, Fabian laughs, "and then I'd do his sides like this", his fingers wriggle assiduously up the rib cage. He gives one final scratch around the neck and pats him on the top of the head. Bune lollops a lick on his cheek and Fabian smiles foolishly, realizes his hands feel just washed, not the usual oily grit after patting a dog.

"Go lie down and eat now."

"Lie down and eat. This is so weird." Fabian steps away and lies down on the grass, curls on his side. He breathes. Oatmeal. He hates oatmeal, but this is only the wholesome kernel, not the viscous slimy part, sun butter melting into caramelizing sugar, glacial milk infused with the generosity of grass. He sits now and looks at Bune, his face quite open.

"Ready?" The wolf starts to vibrate and meld, fur waving and weaving upwards, he lengthens. Fabian squints into the quagmire of movement, tries to focus his eyes, and watches the rushing, upward sprouting. He blinks and there stands Bune replete with wings, rubbing his eyes with his fists and running his leathery hands back through his hair.

"Okay, we should get to work." Behind him on the Membrane sunlight-tinged puffs of cloud drift across a morning sky. "First of all, I need you to tell me the highlights of what you learned in your last assignment, what you see as your real accomplishments, and I will list them on the Membrane so we can talk about them."

"What I learned on summer vacation?"

"Essentially."

Fabian starts to pace, his hands clasped behind his back, head down.

"The first thing you realize, in a, in a *life*, is that shit happens to you and you feel terrible. It's tyranny, shit happens to you right from the beginning, when you are a naked, helpless baby, and the feelings are the worst of it. "*But*," and here he raises both a finger and his eyebrows, "But, I believe I came up with a really brilliant solution. I wrote about it in some of my books, and when they are discovered, I think I will be granted all the esteem that I am due. I wouldn't be surprised in fact, if I go down as one of the great minds of the twentieth century."

"Really? Could you elaborate? What do you mean by 'shit,' and the concurrent feelings, please?"

"Well, you know, pain, simple physical pain for one thing, gas, colic, various infections and inflammation. Then, depending on the reliability of your parents, who knows what you'll get: physical punishment, spanking, pinching, shaking — who can say what level of emotional abandonment they will inflict on you. If you cry out in loneliness and terror, will they come? Hard to say. And through the rest of your life it continues. Shit happens, and you feel pain, loneliness, *sexual frustration*, humiliation, abrasion, a stab in the back, a *kick* to the balls," Fabian demonstrates with gusto, "a punch in the gut. And never, or rarely, the gentle caress, the soothing balm of love."

"Yes," says Bune.

"But I discovered, or rather gathered from the research of others, various plants that produce certain substances. Now these substances, if ingested, create concrete emotions and sensations of their own, and there are a lot of them, a whole menu to choose from. The wise man therefore, although still under the tyranny of fate, can at least decide how he wants to *feel* at any given moment. In that way he can be free, in that way he can at least have some *say*."

"Hmmm, let me try to summarize that . . . " Bune turns toward the Membrane. "Number 1: Avoidance of feeling through botanical interventions." Fabian watches, delighted, as the words project in glowing font on the cloud-filled screen saver.

"Yes, that's it, except don't say 'avoidance of', say, 'liberation from'. And if I can continue along that vein . . . "

"I'm sorry, an interruption." Bune turns his head to the side as if listening to something behind him and to the left. "Ahh . . . " he smiles apologetically. "So sorry." He lifts his right arm into the air and with a pop something materializes in his hand.

"This just in," says Bune, and Fabian stares at a cobalt blue key that winks and twinkles between the angel's thumb and forefinger.

⊹⊹⊹

"My guys can be there any time today. What would work for you?" asks the woman at the other end of the line.

"Really?" Bernie sits parked in front of the school after drop off. "Could they come this morning?"

69

"Absolutely. The city quiets down in the fall. Around Stampede it gets . . . But just give me the address and leave the rest to us. I'll have a dumpster sent over right away. Your father, you said? I can't imagine. My sympathies."

"Yes. Thank you. The house is in Cochrane actually, will that be a problem?"

From the school she drives to a liquor store that piles its cartons on the sidewalk for people to take away. David said he didn't want anything from the house, but Bernie doesn't know what she will find. She wants his books, especially the last one he wrote. She needs to search his study, but even conceptual movement towards that room, and her skin, her insides, pull in the opposite direction. She thinks about drinking something stiff. A shot of medicinal mind-numbing whiskey would come in handy. Little bottles of Jack Daniels in her purse don't seem an option however. Opening the back hatch of the van, she unties Angus from the tether that keeps him in the back. He leaps over the bench seats and settles himself as co-pilot. Bernie loads in the boxes.

As she drives, fog percolates up from the sodden ground to meet the low ceiling of cloud. Rain fell all night and the clouds seem in no hurry to leave. Cars flare up at her on the highway then vanish into the mist as soon as they pass. Bernie pulls into a drive-through coffee place on the edge of town.

"Medium latte please," she says to the dreadlocked boy huddled in his coat behind the take-out window. She drops toonies into his cold fingers and pulls away, the coffee scalding just behind the insulation of the plastic coating. She tries the radio, but nothing seems appropriate, CBC plays a Bartok concerto, cheerful reggae on

CKUA, she hits the button that Eben has set to a station and guttural alternative screaming mixes with the smell of coffee and soggy cardboard and, strangely enough, it seems about right. Pulling into her parents' old driveway, she sees the hulking dumpster already planted on the lawn.

Bernie turns the engine off. Scratching Angus behind his ear, she sips the coffee. The A.D.D. lady, Jeanie, had said they'd be here by ten-thirty. She waits for the biohazard remediation team to show up. Ten forty-five, finally eleven, and a faded maroon Mercury Topaz, rust gnawing the side panels, noses into the driveway and stops. The car sinks into its wheels with a sigh. Two young and very thin men peer out at her from under hoods. She watches as they light cigarettes, take a few drags and then get out. Bernie lowers her window four inches and Angus growls.

"Hello?" The man with the quilted black and red jacket over his tattered hoody approaches her window. He cracks a greying pointy-toothed smile, and rocks from foot to foot, rubbing his hands against his thighs.

"Jeez, it's cold eh? Jeannie said you wanted us to clean out your house? We're from A.D.D . . . " His eyebrows are dark and bushy and, if he should live to be an old man, they could become veritable moustaches.

"You're the 'bioremediation team'?"

"The wha?"

"The, oh never mind. Shouldn't you have protective clothing? I mean, you'll be dealing with bodily fluids!"

"Oh yeah, Jeannie gives us the stuff," and he pulls a pair of yellow kitchen gloves from one pocket, a dust mask on an elastic string from another.

71

"Shouldn't you have a full protective suit . . . ?"

"Oh, don't worry about me, I just take a shower when I get home. This here's Derek," gesturing to his partner, "and I'm Troy. Uh, we're uh, sorry for your loss Ma'am."

Bernie wraps Angus's leash twice around her hand and gets out of the car.

"I'm Bernie and this is Angus."

"I love dogs, I've got a pit-bull cross at home, she's a real sweetie, I named her Crystal," says Troy. He lets Angus sniff his hand and then scratches him behind his ear. Angus actually wags.

"Okay," says Bernie. "Come on, I'll let you in."

Derek walks behind them carrying a ghetto blaster. Bernie finds the plastic rock beside the stairs and tips the key into her hand. She unlocks the door and steps aside so they can go in ahead of her, and the odd mixture of cat box and incense hits her again.

"Wow, what a mess. I mean, we've seen worse though. Where do you want us to start. Where was the body by the way, just so we know?" Bernie starts flicking on lights and trying not to look.

"Anything you want us to save, Ma'am, any keepsakes? Look at that Christmas tree, fuck I don't think he ever took it down . . . "

"The only room I care about is the study. That's where he died, the carpet is the problem, you'll have to rip it out. But I need you to bring everything out from the study and leave it on the porch, so I can go through it before you throw it away. The other rooms, I don't care. I don't want anything." Bernie unclips Angus from his leash and lets him wander the house.

72

"There's some nice furniture here, that looks antique. You sure?" Troy stares at her great-grandmother's mahogany Victorian settee, upholstered in moss velvet. She shakes her head. "Derek, phone Jeanie and tell her to send the big truck."

"No, wait. The old stuff, the antiques, let's leave in the house, but everything else can go. Let me just walk through and look, you could start with the carpets in the living room, what do you do with filthy fake Persian rugs?"

"Dumpster."

Lying on the coffee table she sees various incense-burning vessels, one in particular, a lidded, pierced Aladdin's lamp of brass that she used to play with as a child. Matches, ash, dirty dishes, and prescription bottles. A mouldy, half-eaten apple impaled with a burnt stick of incense. She picks up the dishes and takes them to the kitchen, balancing them on the piles already covering the counter. Bernie starts opening cupboards and at the very top she finds a few of her mother's stoneware casseroles, some tarnished silver jugs. Maybe they should be put away for the kids, the old furniture too. Behind the table her painting hangs crookedly on the wall, a close-up of an organic tangle of plants in a garden. She'd won the grade eleven art award with that one, and she gave it to him for Christmas. "Oh, there's all sorts of stuff in that picture," Fabian says, "gnomes, little sprites; there's more there than meets the eye." Hmm, when you're stoned out of your mind on LSD. She takes it off the wall gingerly, finds newspaper in the living room and wraps it in multiple layers, finds tape, no shortage of tape, and encases it safely like radioactive material. She can't throw it out, perhaps she'll put it in storage. Bernie brings in the boxes from the van, and then walks quickly through the rooms trying to see only obliquely, in case something not too steeped in her father, some remnant of her mother or grandma or David, should be saved for the children.

The guys have the radio playing and are laughing and talking to each other as they roll up and manoeuvre the carpets out the door. In the kitchen she should wash the dishes, and then everything can be donated. Dining room, keep her mother's maple pedestal table and ladder-back chairs for the kids? The old hall chair with the seat that lifts up where she and David, in their childhood, had kept their drenched toques and mittens. The weight of it all. Maybe she'll just sell the furniture. Shed all of this.

"Uh, what do you want to do with the Christmas decorations?" Troy's head pokes around the door frame.

"Sally Ann? Do you guys donate, or will they just go to the dump?"

"I'll put them in boxes if you want, we can take a load to the Women in Need, any furniture you don't want to keep. He spent a shitload on ornaments, holy crap, wish I had . . ."

"Take them for yourself if you want, anything actually, just let me have a look first. You could start on the bedroom and the bathroom, I don't want anything in there just empty them, the clothes and mattress in the dumpster." Bernie walks to the bedroom door and looks into the curtained room piled with dirty clothes to the level of the mattress. He hadn't believed in laundry, only shopping at Costco. In the closet are close to sixty pairs of runners and black slip-on shoes.

"The shoes to the Sally Ann I guess, but I can't go through the clothes." Angus, after eating all the cat food off the floor, plants himself repeatedly in the path of traffic. Bernie takes him outside to the van. Shutting the hatch, she looks over at the pristine clapboard bungalow of Mrs. Gotslieg. The kitchen lights are on. She goes back into the house and starts on the piles of dishes, the cups spackled with dried Metamucil are the worst, she fills both sides of the sink and puts them all in to soak, fills the dishwasher with the first load and turns it on. He seemed only to have eaten three things, London Broils, pre-cooked stuffed mashed potatoes, and cereal. And coffee. In one cupboard she found six containers of Metamucil. The freezer compartment in the fridge barely shuts and a frozen potato falls like a brick on the top of her foot. She is hopping around swearing when Troy walks by with a heap of clothes in his arms. "Please," she says, "at the end of the day take all this food home if you want it." Derek follows behind him, his usually subaudible voice cracked and husky, "This shit man, I can't believe the street value . . . " Seeing Bernie, he recedes back into his hood as they go out the kitchen door.

After she finishes the dishes the guys start on the study, carrying everything out onto the back porch, the desk, a blue plastic storage box of cables and techno-logical detritus, two squat filing cabinets.

"Could you put the computer over by my van?" she asks, as they come out carrying the monitor and the tower. Digging through the computer cables, she finds four memory sticks that she zips into an outside pocket of her purse. The filing cabinet holds manila folders, old medical and financial paperwork, and stuffed in the back she finds the plush toys she'd sewn him. A zebra with a string mane, a passable replica of the Velveteen Bunny, a black bear with button eyes. When had she done these? Probably junior high after she'd taken sewing in Home Economics. She remembers Fabian in the kitchen pretending to be one of his favourite personas, the whiney "Little Brother Tim," holding the stuffed rabbit against his chest and stroking it, talking in that nasal voice. Bernie cringing that her friend should see this. How many fathers elicit stuffed animals from their adolescent daughters? He'd never asked actually, she'd just known all along who the baby was.

"I don't need any of this. Chuck it all, dumpster, Women in Need, whatever." Angus barks hysterically in the van. He must see something.

She looks up to the toes of the coulee at the far stretch of the yard. Sitting in the willow scrub, a coyote studies her for a long moment, then trots silently north and vanishes into a gully. They still use the old pathway. How many generations of coyote have followed that trail? Maybe even before the first tarpapered shanty of Cochrane. She used to wake at night to their jittering howls, was lulled back to sleep by their family singing, their intimate talk. Bernie puts her hands on the small of her back, stretches her hips forward. The fog clears. Through the cloud she sees the circle of the sun.

She sticks her head into the living room; Derek is bent over picking up prescription bottles with his skinny hands. He shakes each one and puts it carefully in the cardboard box. "Incredible," he mutters.

"You guys need lunch?"

Derek stops midshake.

"Yah, that would be great!" says Troy.

"How about Vietnamese subs? I know a place in Cochrane. Chicken? Beef? Hot pepper, no hot pepper?"

When Bernie comes back, thin sunlight is brightening if not warming the deck. She bought them each two subs and a Coke.

"Come out here and eat guys." They hold the box between them, Troy running his hands through the plastic vials like a child sifting pebbles in the surf. "Why don't you bring that outside, tell me about what you're finding," they look at her, startled, putting the box down behind them on the table. Coming onto the deck, they reach for the food. "Jesus, go wash your hands first, *bodily fluids*, you could get E. coli poisoning!" Bernie mutters in disbelief as they head for the bathroom. She sets the Adirondack chairs back on their feet, then positions three to face the coulee. The guys shuffle out and sit down. Derek and Troy pull back their hoods and take their sandwiches.

"Wow, thanks. People don't usually buy us lunch," says Troy.

"Yeah, thanks!" says Derek.

Bernie watches sideways as Derek inhales his sub. His blond hair is shaved close and a white scar runs through the stubble behind his ear and around to his occipital lobe. She studies a tattoo on his neck. The box lies brimming in front of her feet. She waits until they are halfway through their second sandwich then she pulls her chair around part way so she can see them better.

"So, can you tell me about, I mean, what was my dad taking?"

"Mmmph?" says Troy chewing fast to pull the overhanging cilantro and shredded carrot past his lips. He swallows. "Your dad was *The Man*, eh Derek?"

"Incredible, he must have had six doctors he was shopping to get this much . . . " he leans forward and roots through the box pulling out vials. "Look at this, Tylenol Threes, they're not too hard to get, good old 'Doors and Fours.' Whadaya call Percocet?"

"Tango and Cash," says Troy.

"*Oxycontin* eighty milligrams! Man, that's gold! He could have sold that on the street for what?"

"Dollar a mill easy, and there were thirty tabs in a bottle? He couldn't have been buying it, he must have been doing the doctor shopping himself."

"So what sort of drugs are they? Do they do different things?"

"Mainly the same stuff, but just stronger."

"What kind of stuff?"

"They're all from opium . . . " Troy turns to his friend.

"Opiates." Derek leans forward and paws through the box. "He did some uppers too, Dexedrine, bennies, but not so much."

Bernie looks at the chicken satay sub wrapped in red-and-white checked paper. She should eat something, so she unwraps it.

"What's so great about opiates?'

Troy looks at her out of his left eye, his head tipped back as he drinks the Coke. He splutters midswallow. "What's so great about it? I don't do it too much now,

78

eh Derek? You gotta be careful chasing the Dopamine Dragon."

"Yeah, you don't want to be chasing the rush man. But your dad must have paced himself, maybe he took breaks. If you don't snort it or smoke, you can go a long time."

"Okay, but how does it make you feel?" The guys glance down at the last of their sandwiches in their laps, smiling. Troy pushes Derek's shoulder.

"Imagine this, it's the middle of the winter somewhere, and you know it's really *fucking* cold outside, but you're *inside,* in a cabin in front of a roaring fire, wrapped in a blanket with the girl of your dreams. It's like that," says Derek in his husky voice.

"Warm and tingly all over, you're totally safe and relaxed, not a care in the world."

"It's like being a baby in your momma's arms."

"Yeah, it's like that."

Bernie nods. "Okay" she says. She can't stomach more so she picks the cilantro and the carrots out and eats that. "Why don't you do it very often now?" "So addictive man! Gets too expensive, Angie got sick of me being stoned or asleep."

Derek pipes up, "Gives you wicked constipation too, and when you don't have it you feel like shit, nervous all the time." Bernie exhales.

"Okay, well. Interesting to know." I guess that explains the Metamucil, she thinks. "How much longer will it take to clear out the rest of the house?" She looks at her watch, it says two o'clock. She will have to phone Peter to pick the kids up from school.

They finish at five, leaving the house still dirty but empty except for her grandmother's furniture.

"So, Jeanie will send you the bill," says Troy "and if you need help with the basement, we can come back." He watches her with his recessed eyes, waiting. She has no cash in her purse, but that's just as well. They'd probably spend it on "Doors and Fours".

"I want to tip you guys. You've been great, but I've got no cash. Could you follow me into Cochrane?" Bernie drives with the wheezing Topaz trailing her, but she doesn't go to a cash machine. Instead she stops at Mark's Work Warehouse and takes them shopping. They pick out new hoodies, and she gets them socks, gloves, and down vests. Troy picks an orange one and Derek navy blue, "don't want to be too matchy matchy," he says. Outside on the sidewalk she hands them their clothes as they scuff their feet on the concrete, thank her, and shake hands.

"Take care guys and keep warm. Winter's coming." Bernie gets into her van and sits for a minute with Angus's snout resting on her shoulder. In the rear-view mirror, she watches them rooting through their shopping bags. Then she starts the van and drives home.

"Shall we go in, then?" Bune inserts the blue key into the vibrating apparition of the door projected on the Membrane.

"But the Dark! If you puncture the Membrane, we'll . . . " Bune pushes the door, which swings away and opens to black. The fluffy clouds keep progressing left. When they reach the door frame, they vanish but then re-emerge in perfect time on the other side.

"We'll fall!"

"I can fly, remember, I'll carry you. I am eager to see the place where your greatest achievement was brought to fruition. What did you call it?"

"Liberation from feeling . . . " mumbles Fabian. "Why can't we just stay here, and I'll tell you?"

"A little field trip will be invigorating and informative. Come!" and with a swoop Bune scoops Fabian, clasping him in arms of steel against his chest, and steps to the threshold. "Whoopsy!" and he falls backwards through the door. Fabian screams and squeezes his eyes tight shut. They are falling, then the angel rotates so Fabian is face first into the abyss. He must not look. *Whump*, the wings open and catch them. He listens to their slow confident sweep; he and Bune seem to hover, taking lazy curves and dips like flotsam on the water.

"Open your eyes now, I have you. You can't fall."

"I don't want to look. Where are we? In the Black, in the ocean? I'm not a good swimmer."

"No, in your old home. You are perfectly safe. Open your eyes and see."

Fabian finally looks and jerks so violently that even Bune is surprised and has to change his grip.

"Get out of my house!" screams Fabian. "Don't touch my stuff, get them out of here, get them out!" he twists back to look up at Bune.

"Easy, you're dead. You don't need any of that now."

"They're stealing my pills! You have no idea what I went through to get those." They are floating somewhere close to the ceiling though the ceiling seems higher than Fabian remembers. Two mangy vandals in hoodies are moving through the living room picking up medicine vials and putting them in a box that is now almost full.

A woman with curly red blond hair comes into the living room and talks to them.

"Bernie! That's my daughter. Why is she speaking to them, why is she allowing this?"

"I think they are cleaning out your house, since you *are* dead."

"Oh," Fabian sighs deeply. "I guess so." Then brightening, "they won't find anything anyhow. I used them all up. Now she shows up, eh? She's been gone for seven years, but now she shows up for the pickings."

"You were not in contact with her?"

"No, she left. They all leave."

"Hmm, let's see," says Bune. The living room begins to shift and flash, furniture changes and moves, days and nights fly by, people walk in and out, children play a piano, sprawl on the carpet with Monopoly, lounge in chairs reading. The flashing stops. Sunlight and order fill the room, plants grow on bookshelves, and a woman with glossy black hair vacuums a carpet intricate as a Persian garden. A black cat sleeps in a patch of sun on the couch.

"Oh God, I don't want to see her. That's Margaret, that's my wife. That's the rug we brought home from India."

"She left then?"

"Yes, the children grew up and she left. She said she couldn't handle my depressions, what she called my 'paranoia'. She took the bloody rug too."

"Let's fast forward a bit." More flashing and a new era of gloom and mess, the curtains closed, only the cat and Fabian come and go from couch to kitchen, to bathroom and bedroom, then a flurry of tidying, a new black leather sofa is moved in, a large potted fig tree, the curtains are opened. On the couch Fabian and a woman roll in an embrace. The living room seems to breathe the light and a rhythm of regular life for a time, some speeding days. Through all the seasons the occasional red blonde frizz of Bernie's hair. But then darkness and mess descend again.

"Who was that other woman? The gentle quiet one."

"My girlfriend Serena, I thought she was too insecure to ever leave me, but she did. She started going to counselling." Bune zooms forward in time, then backwards as if searching for something in this piling mess, a clammy darkness only punctuated by Fabian and the cat.

"I can't even find your daughter at this point. She stopped coming to visit . . . "

"Yes, it shows that even the ties of blood don't prove reliable. Margaret only married me, but I was Bernie's *father*." They hover now and look down. Fabian sleeps on the couch, the cat curls in his customary spot at his feet, but no sunlight warms him.

"So, I'm finding it hard to locate this pinnacle of achievement you speak of so glowingly. Too be honest, your home seems gloomy and chaotic, grim even. Certainly, you were not much of a housekeeper . . . "

Fabian laughs.

"But that's the brilliant thing about it. I have hidden it. It has nothing to do with mundane physical reality. I carried inside of me a golden alternate place to dwell. I met Margaret in college, and I discovered my great insight around the same time."

"Well let's go down there. You must show me." They slowly rotate from parallel to horizontal and then descend until their feet hit the soft layers of Costco carpets, gritty with kitty litter and coffee grounds. Bune walks to the couch and leans over the sleeping rotund and balding man. "Where exactly?" he looks over his shoulder at Fabian.

"It felt like about here," Fabian rubs his solar plexus in a circular motion. Bune stretches out his hand and lays it flat on the man's sweater-covered chest, and then his hand descends until it disappears up to the wrist. For a moment he waits, feeling around and then slowly he pulls it back out, leaving the sweater unscathed and intact. He holds aloft in his hand a glowing orb, shooting out intermittent sparks of pink and gold static electricity.

"Yes! That's it! Now I see what it looks like. It looks just how it felt! So beautiful, so pure, and so faithful. I could always return there."

Bune sits on an ottoman, his wings dangling behind him and his legs outstretched. He studies the orb.

"It's very pretty." Gently he jiggles the ball, and then lightly, sitting more erect, he begins to toss it from hand to hand. Fabian is perched on the arm of the sofa to the left of the cat.

"Be respectful! Don't chuck it around. What if you drop it!"

But Bune hums quietly to himself as he performs his little juggling act. In one hand now, he sets it spinning in a circle, catching and re-catching. Fabian gnashes his teeth and growls. Bune switches to the other hand.

"I just wonder . . ." Now he chucks it high in the air and with each catch when it comes down, the orb deflects a bit, distorts into first a flattened oval and then something more irregular. Bune gives it a really good chuck and it hits the ceiling, *smack*. Fabian roars in rage as the orb explodes into a mass of tentacles and erratic tongues. The thing falls into Bune's hands with a wet squelch and gives off a long, low whine.

"Ah, I thought so," says Bune. "It was initially in its defensive position, like a hedgehog, but now it has uncurled so we can see the true form." He puts it down on the floor and wipes his hands on his cloud gown.

"What have you done to it? You've broken my beautiful orb, now it looks all . . ." The thing is moving, amoeba-like across the gritty rug, its various tongues take turns acting like the foot of a snail, while the tentacles wave and search about, sniffing and snuffling desperately.

"It appears to have no vision, but an excellent sense of smell."

"*Mehhehheh,*" moans the thing. The tentacles envelope but then spit out bits of kitty litter as they come to them. Fabian creeps higher onto the back of the couch, never taking his eyes off it. The cat wakes up with a hiss and runs into the kitchen.

"Well it doesn't like to eat kitty litter. Ah, yes, it can smell its host now, it's making a bee line." The thing tumbles forward, eagerly tripping on its assorted tongues until it reaches the man's hand hanging over the edge of the sofa. Several tentacles rise, pull back and then slap forward with certainty, suctioning onto his wrist and knuckles.

"*Mehhhhh*" it whines, pulling the hand angrily. "*Meh*" The man opens his eyes as his hand is dragged away from the couch by the insistent amoeba, his arm stretches and finally he falls on the rug, gets to his hands and knees, and begins to crawl. Finally, he stands. The thing slimes its way up his leg, wraps tentacles around his abdomen, pussyfoots to the centre of his chest, and with a burp burrows out of sight.

"Euew!" says Bune. He walks to the couch and picks up Fabian, holding him in the crook of his arm, but facing out so he can see. The man stumbles around the living room searching. Whenever he finds a prescription bottle, he shakes it, but all are empty. At last, under a couch cushion he locates one that is full. He opens it with shaking hands and puts a tablet under his tongue, sits down on the couch, head in hands, and then reaches for a box of matches and a stick of incense on the coffee table. He lights it, jams the unlit end into a half-eaten apple, and then lies down on the couch. He rolls over, his back to the room.

"Well! Have you had enough then? Do you want to go?"

Fabian nods wordlessly, yes.

When Bernie returns to the house, lemon cleaner and residual incense mutate in the air. Jeannie sent over a cleaning crew to wash things down yesterday, and now all the surfaces breathe and flex, a little raw, the particulate skin of Fabian's last seven years so suddenly stripped away. Bernie opens cupboards to witness their emptiness. He is not here, not here, not here. With nothing to investigate, Angus lies down with a grunt, rolls over and sprawls on his back. A soft wind blows through the kitchen door. She thinks of her studio in the backyard, waiting to be sorted out. But she will go to the basement to see what has to be done next and then she will leave.

"Come on Angus." Bernie walks to the eight-panelled door in the wall to the left of the range. She twists the pressed glass doorknob and pushes, stretches her arm into the dark to find the beaded chain on the wall to her left, pulls and hears the familiar 'ca chunk', the tiny clatter when she lets go of the chain. The bulb flickers into action and Angus scrambles down the stairs into the mildewy dank. As she descends, Bernie trails her hand over the cemented stone foundation. When they were dating Peter had waxed ecstatic about these footings, triple the width of a modern foundation to compensate for the instability of piled river rock. At the bottom she walks and opens the small door to the cold room built under the stairs. Pulls another light cord. Empty, except for a box of canning jars and a straw broom worn to an angle. She turns off the light. Pivoting, Bernie walks into the basement proper, trying to remember where the next light switch is, and bangs face first into some implacable barrier.

"What? What on Earth?" She slides her hands over papery smoothness to left and right, over her head. A new wall stretches where once had been open space. Angus bounces around in the dark snuffling. "What are you doing Angus? This is so weird, I don't remember . . . " Bernie returns to the foot of the stairs and finds the light switch, the dog scratches frantically at the bottom corner of the wall where the bumpy foundation left a gap for a mouse. She sits down on the fourth step and stares. He must have erected this rough two-by-four partition. Drywall panels extend floor to ceiling and wall-to-wall, jaggedly cut and screwed to the wood. Scrawled in thick black Sharpie. Two words. Her father's messy capitals: FRAMING WHITEY.

"Framing whitey?" Bernie walks to the wall and kneels down and examines the gobs of dried Bulldog Adhesive that squished out when he set the bottom plate onto the concrete. Above she sees more grey goop between the top plate and the floor joists. He glued it; he glued the whole frame together instead of using nails or screws. Classic.

In the dim light she opens the camera app on her cell phone and takes a picture of the wall. She attaches the picture to a text and sends it to her brother:

"David, I cleared the main floor but look what I found in the basement. Now to puncture the chamber of the tomb. I feel like Howard Carter discovering King Tut, but not so hopeful."

ᴑ-ᴑ-ᴑ

Fabian lies curled in a ball on the turf and won't unroll. Squatting on his heels, Bune watches and waits. He rises, walks to Fabian and gently pushes him, his calloused toe tentative against Fabian's satin skin.

"Leave me. Just leave me alone."

"It will help if we talk. Come on, sit up. Time keeps speeding by. Look at the Membrane, the sunsets." He nudges him more firmly with his foot, rolling him over on his side. Fabian sits but turns his back on the fiery sky.

"What bothers you the most about this um, your greatest um, achievement . . . ?"

"I never thought an angel would employ sarcasm. What sort of angel are you anyway? What sort of fucking afterlife experience is this? I want a union, I want . . . "

Fabian drops his head between his knees and his shoulders heave their dry sobs. "I want real tears!"

"I did not mean to employ sarcasm. Seeing the truth hurts I know, when you thought . . . "

Fabian stares into the black and Bune waits. Finally, he rotates and looks up at the demon, his baby face bitter.

"It's easy for you I suppose, you don't have to deal with the *real* world, the frustrations, the demands of a degenerating body, scarred psyches, out of whack neurotransmitters, abandonment issues and attachment disorders. Easy for you to judge, to say I should have been stronger."

Bune squats beside Fabian, and then sits cross-legged. He reaches out his arm to put it around Fabian, but lets it drop.

"I was mortal too, you know, long ago. Mortal for eons, and the mistakes and crimes I committed could fill many books. I do not judge you. Your last assignment was daunting, you were sent in ill-equipped. But now you fully understand suffering through addiction, so in that light you actually succeeded."

"What are you telling me? The whole thing was a set-up, my free will an illusion?"

"Through free will you might have learned the lesson an easier way, pulled out sooner, sought help. But you confused yourself. The addiction was not the door you sought, but the cage that held you."

Fabian rotates glumly, faces the cloud-infested screen saver.

"I thought I was steering the ship, I thought I was so damn smart!"

Bune stands, then bends and takes the small face in his hands. He smooths the towhead eyebrows with his craggy thumbs.

"Very good. That's not easy to admit."

Fabian twists out of his grasp, jumps to his feet.

"I'm not a *complete* idiot though. I admit the last phase of my life was largely a mistake, but in my twenties and thirties I *saw*. I really looked into the very eye of truth, the core of the universe. I wrote a hell of a good book about those discoveries, and it received overwhelming critical acclaim. If anything, I peaked too soon. Yes, that's it; I was ruined by premature success. Many great artists struggle with that. Destroy themselves."

Bune clutches his head.

"God help me. Here slow down, come back a minute. You raced through the first lesson too quickly. You admitted that your life was out of control . . . that you weren't 'steering the ship', that ego blinded you . . . "

"I know what you are doing. This is a 'life review'. I'm supposed to take stock of all my mistakes and say I'm sorry. Well I don't see the point. It's not like I could go back, could I? I think you're a sadist, I think the 'Big Picture' in fact is a sadistic punishing plan. What I did wrong I did for understandable reasons, battered by my childhood and a fucked up societal agenda, you're not going to make me grovel step by step through every . . . "

"Let me know when you've spent yourself." Bune extends his right hand into the air and materializes a fuming cigarette. He puffs away busily until he notices Fabian staring, jaw dropped. "You make me remember smoking. Are you done now?" He spits the butt into the air where it disperses. "You don't have to say you are sorry, but merely understand. I believe we covered your 'greatest achievement.' Now I need to know your greatest shame."

"Like I said, there is no shame, considering, under the circumstances . . . "

"Please, just *tell* me. Think. I'll give you something in exchange. What would you like? I can return anything to you. Ah, I know, I'll give you back your tears."

Fabian stands up and walks away into the dark, his little ass disdainful.

"I won't be coerced or bought out or duped! Fuck, I've got nowhere to go, I've got all the time in the world!"

"Neaah! Gammrrrrr. Shaa!" Fabian jumps a bit but keeps on walking. Two extra heads shoot out of Bune's shoulders, rotate wildly and growl and clack. Fabian glances back and stares, then carries on.

"All the time, all the time in the world. Your pyrotechnics don't scare me."

Bune tips his angel face to the ceiling, lets out a shriek, and becomes lion and eagle. All rippling muscle and scaly leg, he curls in his talons and springs, pins Fabian's neck to the turf with black spurs, his thrashing legs silenced with leaden paws.

"Tell me," he hisses into Fabian's ear, "tell me your greatest shame, or I'll shake you until your brains curdle. *Tell me!*" He bears down but the boy's face disappears into the turf with the weight. With his beak he pulls back on the silky hair, and Fabian comes up, grass in teeth. "*Speak!*"

"D-D-D-D-David!"

"Ahhh, yes." Behind them a distinct "boing" resounds. The griffon looks over and sees a pearlescent football lying on the ground. *"And?"*

"B-B-B-Bernie. Bernadette."

"Right again." A "ping" rings out and another package arrives, both nest in hollows on the ground. Perhaps they are seeds, hypocotyl, epicotyl, cotyledon, ready to sprout. Or eggs, tucked in flippers, or vestigial limbs, all tightly wrapped in a transparent uterine skin.

☙ ☙ ☙

The children are sleeping, the last pages of *Harriet the Spy* concluded, and Angus let out for a final pee. Now he twitches in the corner on his dog bed, trotting through some canine dream. Bernadette lies under the insufficient summer duvet. Time to switch to the warmer quilt, but she doesn't get up. The bizarre basement churns in her head. Then at the front of the house the opening and closing of the door, Peter! He rustles around in the fridge, then goes upstairs and opens Eben's door for a moment. Downstairs he checks on the other three, and then his tired step down the hallway. Quietly he walks into the bedroom.

"You're back!"

"I thought you'd be sleeping."

"I'm cold. I can't stop thinking." She sits up and turns on the lamp by the bed and looks at the haggard remains of her husband. "Tell me Terminal D is out for tender. You look exhausted."

Peter runs his hands through his hair making it stand on end, he flares his eyes at her then leans across the bed for a kiss.

"Done, thank God. If AutoCAD hadn't crashed this morning, I would have been home by six, but we finally got it out." He goes into the bathroom and she listens to the drumming of the shower, then he returns in a cloud of steam, hairy and towelling down, turns off the light, and crawls into bed.

"Come here," and he pulls her backwards into the curve of his chest.

"How was your day? Did you go back?" He tucks the frizzy mass of her hair around and under her head, so it won't go up his nose and presses his face into her neck.

"It just keeps getting weirder."

"Those guys from A.D.D. weren't there again, were they? Have you moved the key? They know how to get in now. I don't like you being there on your own."

"No, no, nothing to do with them. Some cleaning people came yesterday. I let them in and the key is on my key chain now. I didn't leave it in the rock."

"So what's weird about it?"

"Well you won't believe this, I went downstairs, and my dad must have built a wall blocking off the whole basement. He wrote "Framing Whitey" in felt pen, big letters. I have no idea what that means, and he didn't put in a door. He sealed the basement as if it was a sarcophagus or something." Now lapped in the heat radiating from Peter, the dysfunctional labyrinth recedes from her and she starts to feel drowsy.

"Weirder and weirder. What do you plan to do?"

"Hmm, do? I just need a sledgehammer, we have one, don't we?"

"Oh no, uh uh. You're not going in there alone, not until I know what's behind that wall. Remember the German Shepherd he shot, when did he do that?"

"When I was five. His name was Gus and he'd bitten the postman. My dad took him out to the country and shot him. He told my mother he could purge his own aggressions somehow by doing that, that the dog was a vessel for my father's baser instincts."

"His gun collection always worried me. There was no reason for having them, not like he was a hunter."

"No, just more of his paranoid self-defense."

"Then the "secret Santa" packages for the kids, a continuation of the gun theme, and who knows where his mind went after you cut him off."

"By the end, I think he was too addicted to be dangerous. He never took any action. He just liked to picture himself as some sort of subversive hero. He was a coward maybe or . . . no there was a politeness . . . he would have been embarrassed somehow to actually go postal."

"That's not so reassuring. Tomorrow is Saturday and we can go together. I don't want you alone in there until I know what's behind that wall. Eben can watch the little kids." He pulls her in more snugly. "I'm so tired I could drop."

"So much for forging a relationship of trust." Fabian tentatively pats the welts on his neck. Bune is examining the two packages. He straightens up and glowers. "You could have offered more options, rather than resorting to violence . . . "

"Believe me, it's for your own good, because actually you *don't* have all the time in the world. Actually, your time on Corridor Nine is very, very finite. You will find something *has* been restored to you though, not that you deserve it. I need a time out. I'm going for a walk. You stay here, and don't touch these packages." He runs his hands through his greying tufts. "You seriously exhaust me. Oh, and while you wait you might as well have dinner." Bune strides off until he disappears around the distant curve of the Membrane. When he is quite gone Fabian crawls forward on hands and knees, approaching the eggs. The flattened features of his two children, rounded, indistinct suggestions of their future selves, press into folded arms and legs, the curve of small backs. He closes his eyes.

"Go away, go away." He gets to his feet and runs into the dark and bounces for a long time. When he stops, his legs feel like trembling rubber and his breath comes in rhythmic gasps. His body thrums with the familiar release of lactic acid, so nostalgic an ache that if only he could, he would weep. Contrite, he sits cross-legged and thinks, and in a little while he remembers. Breathe in the ether of the turf. What does it offer tonight? And obediently he rolls onto his side and inhales.

An Asian broth infused with lemongrass, ginger, and scallions. There is nothing else on the menu, so he breathes for awhile longer until full. When Bune returns from his lap around Corridor Nine, he finds Fabian sleeping, curled up in the dark.

In the nook off the kitchen, Moira and Louis sit wedged together.

"It's not fair, I am not watching any more Minecraft. You said after the last one we could play Animal Jam." Mo lunges for the mouse, swivelling the rolling chair. Louis, his eyes still trained on the screen but rotated so he has to look over his shoulder, paws blindly for the mouse and finally grabs it. Moira opens her mouth wide, leans forward and anchors her teeth tentatively around his bicep.

"Ish my turn. You promised,"

"In a sec, just let me finish this one. We played yours the whole time yesterday . . . "

Moira thinks of the documentaries she has watched, the wolves tearing at carcasses, and tightens her jaw muscles a little more, gives her head the sideways death shake as if breaking the neck of a rabbit. Louis lets out a roar, and the discordant sound penetrates Eben's earbuds, as he lies on the couch listening to The Offspring. He rolls onto his back and contemplates investigating, when another muffled off-beat squeal breaks through, and finally he pulls the earbuds out and sits up. Screaming. How serious a screaming? The twins bang about around the corner, the swivel chair slides.

"Mommy! Mommy! Oiw, *oiw, oiwwwww!*" The scream hits a certain octave. Eben catapults off the couch. He runs to the nook and swings around the corner.

"Stop! *Stop! Moira.* What are you doing?" Mo returns from the arctic tundra, tastes soggy flannel in her mouth, and releases her grip. Lou howls and scrabbles at his arm.

96

"Jesus Mo, you can't bite! You're not a baby. What the hell!" Eben leans over the back of the chair, pulls his little brother to safety, and sits him on the floor.

"I want Mommy, I want Mommy." Lou is really sobbing. Eben looks at the arm, no blood through the shirt at least. He tries to pull the shirt off over his head, but the buttoned cuffs foil him and he has to pull the shirt down, unbutton, and start over. Mo hunkers down and peers over the arm of the swivel chair.

"Look at this Mo. It's all red and there's going to be a huge bruise. What the fuck? Go get an icepack." Lou topples sideways on the floor, still crying.

"I want Momma . . . " Eben looks down at him, bends over and gives him a rough pat on the back. "Mommaaaa!" Eben pats again, rolls his eyes and kneels, getting his cheek against the floor so he's peering into Louis' sobbing face.

"Lou, stop! Lou you want some Ichiban?" Louder, "Ichiban Lou?" Moira arrives with a gel pack from the freezer.

"Ichiban?" Louis sits up. "Momma said she wasn't buying any more," a snivel, an inhalation of snot. "She said it was junk."

"I found a whole case." He takes the gel pack from Mo. "Bring me some masking tape." He pulls the shirt back over Lou's head and once he's got the sleeves on, he folds the gel pack around his little brother's bicep. Mo hands him tape and Eben straps everything in place. She hovers somewhere behind, and Eben reaches back and grabs her sweatshirt, pulls her around to face him, partially lifting her off the floor, her hair cockeyed around the skinny little face.

"Say you're sorry."

"I'm sorry! I didn't mean to. I was doing the lupus neck crack . . . " she trails off. "Are you telling Mom?"

"*I'm* telling Mom!" snivels Lou.

"No, no one's telling Mom. Remember what Dad said? We have to help her out for awhile, 'go easy on her'? She's got enough to think about with her crazy dad dying."

Lola comes into the kitchen.

"What's all the screaming?"

"Mo bit Lou, but don't tell Mom. It's no big deal." Eben goes down to the basement and finds the crate of Ichiban beside the packs of paper towels and toilet paper. He looks briefly at the sticky note that reads Don't Eat. For Foodbank, cracks open the cardboard lid and takes out two of the cups, then thinks better of it, returns them and picks up the whole box. It should fit under his bed. He walks back upstairs and boils the kettle. Lola digs around in the fridge. She pulls the plastic container of mealworms and sawdust out of the cheese drawer and shakes it.

"If they aren't wiggling very much do you think they're still edible? Hey, can I have an Ichiban?"

⊷⊷⊷

Peter and Bernie sit in the driveway. The car makes ticking noises as the engine cools. The leaves are all down now but most of them blew into the coulee.

"Does the old lady still live next door?"

"Mrs. Gotslieg? I told you, she has his cat."

"We should go say hello."

"I've not been able to face that." They get out of the car and walk across the crunching gravel. He looks around at the poplars.

"So many memories here, eh?"

Bernie curls her hand inside his palm.

'Oh, we need the sledgehammer."

Peter goes back to get it, and Bernie walks up the steps and unlocks the door. Her watch says noon; at home the kids probably sit glued to the computer. Before her father had detonated there had been "media days" and "non-media days" and time limits. She feels guilty; she has to start being more present. She steps into her father's kitchen, where the sun streams in but the air still stinks. She walks from room to room opening every window.

"We should take this old furniture home, the Victorian settee, and the hall chair with the coat hooks," Peter says from the living room.

"I can't. They remind me of him, but my great-grandmother brought them with her when she came west from Ontario. I don't know what to do."

"We could save the furniture for the kids then. They don't know. Rent a storage locker. Actually there's room in the garage."

"That would work, I guess. Come on, let's get this done."

Peter pulls two camping headlamps out of his coat pocket before they descend the stairs.

"I doubt he installed lights in the sarcophagus."

"We look like spelunkers."

With a dull thwack the hammer hits the drywall and punches a neat hole through the word 'Framing'. Peter hits the wall a few more times and then kicks out a larger opening with his foot, tears off pieces still attached by the paper, and sticks his head in.

"Weird."

"Let me see."

"It's all white."

"Go in so I can see." Bernie pushes him forward. She steps through and their beams of light skitter across a new wall two metres in front of them. At first Bernie thinks this one is built of long bricks painted white, and then she realizes they are books. Each book identical, the size of the yellow pages directory, stacked on their sides, from the concrete slab to the stained floor joists above them. The untitled spines all face out.

Peter reaches up and pulls one off the top of the stack and hands it to Bernie, heavy in her hands. *Framing Whitey* in big block letters, and a little smaller, "by Fabian Macomber." She flips through the first pages and can't find a publisher or copyright date. Bernie reaches up and pulls down another, *Framing Whitey* and another and another.

"If you were looking for his writing, I guess we've found it! I wonder how far back this goes. Did he fill the whole basement? Your dad never believed in moderation."

"He must have self-published and had them printed. What am I going to do with a basement full, totally full of what? His manifesto? Maybe he thought I would distribute them?" Bernie laughs.

"What?"

"Oh this just reminds me. When I was a kid and my dad used to fart, instead of 'excuse me', he would say, 'This is my letter to the world that never wrote to me . . .' It's a quote. From Emily Dickenson." The weight of the book hums in her hands and she lays it on the concrete. "I don't want to read this today. Let's go home."

"The pyramids were built like this you know, a massive pile of stone blocks. The actual passage and chambers only make up ten percent of the total volume. Well it seems benign enough, as long as he didn't hide Anthrax between the pages. As long as there's no 'inner sanctum'." He picks the book off the floor, Bernie ducks through the hole in the drywall and they head up the stairs.

"I wonder if A.D.D. would clear out several tons of books, even if there are no bodily fluids involved."

"They were dodgy, I'll ask around at work and see if anyone knows a better company."

"No don't. I liked them actually. They were fine. They just looked a bit rough." Upstairs Bernie shuts the windows. The sun radiates the heat of August but even in the afternoon the chill of night hangs in the air. These last days of Indian summer are the quietest of the year.

Driving east on the highway back to Calgary, they crest the Cochrane hill and pass the sign for the St. Francis Retreat.

"Do you feel like you're done now?"

"What do you mean?"

"Well you said you needed 'proof of his insanity' so you could stop feeling guilty. I think the manifesto-filled basement qualifies, don't you?"

"I suppose so. Now I just have to make myself read it."

"Hey, you know what we *didn't* find?"

"What?"

"His guns. I wonder where he put all his guns?"

⊷⊷⊷

"This exercise involves Seeing the Other. Once you have accomplished that we can move on to lesson three."

"What was lesson one?"

"Well you didn't master it completely and we will have to review some more, but you realized that your life was out of control . . . You admitted you needed help."

"I still don't understand. You're telling me that the lessons I learn here I can carry with me into my next life, my next assignment. What if I just forget them, like I apparently did all those other times?"

"You were noncompliant on previous occasions. Never have I met a soul so pigheaded. But yes, the lessons you learn here should stay with you. They will feel like muscle memory, if you understand me."

Fabian and Bune stand with the packages lying a metre in front of them. Behind the eggs the Membrane does another riff on 'autumnal afternoon', golden cheer and cerulean sky, but he thinks only of the bull's eye map and the elusive sparkle that marks the exit. The eggs flex inside their iridescent rubbery skins.

Fabian gives Bune a squeamish look.

"What do I have to do with them?"

"First we unwrap them."

"I hate babies. What then, change their diapers? Breast feed?"

"No, just *see* them." Bune bends over and examines the more masculine egg. "There should be a rip strip here somewhere, ah yes." He pulls delicately on a bit of filament at the end of the egg and the whole contraption comes apart like a cardboard tube of Pillsbury Crescent Rolls, baby flesh spilling out.

"Yuck . . . "

"Just wait, direct contact is not called for." The wrapper rises up as if pulled by an invisible hand, some gentle tugs from Bune to dislodge from the soft weight of the entity. The baby momentarily divulges limbs as the wrapper pulls free, before contracting to its habitual tuck. The covering stretches, expanding in two-dimensional space. It forms a taut rectangular screen, blocking their view down to the turf. "The barrier simulates conditions on Earth, metaphorically at least. Now your job is to look through the screen and just accurately *see* the person behind."

"What person?"

"Do not dismiss the germ of existence. Every life form sprouts from there but also carries that kernel within. Look through the screen and describe what you see."

Fabian squints at the opalescent surface and makes out his own reflection.

"How can I look through a mirror?"

⟳⟐⟳

"We're back! Hello, turn off all media devices." No response. "Hello? Where are my children?" Bernie finds the twins in the nook and pushes the power button on the back of the computer before they realize what she has done. Eben sits up from the couch.

"Hi Ebe. Were the kids good? Any plans today?"

"Fine nothing mrf . . . ."

"What? Where are you going?"

"My room . . . homework."

"Where's my Lola? Lola!" The girl comes into the kitchen, the hedgehog encircled by her hands. Angus dances about sniffing and Cynthia twitches and clicks, her spines rising. Peter peels a banana at the counter and watches the dog rotate around his daughter and the prickly mammal. He picks up his foot and boots Angus in the bum.

"Get! Get out of here." Angus looks offended, tucks his tail, and leaves the kitchen.

"Don't kick him Daddy!"

"Angus will hunt any little animal Lola. He won't understand if I just explain nicely, it's the law of the pack."

Bernie opens the fridge and pokes around.

"We're out of everything again. How did that happen?" She straightens up and looks out the windows at the limpid sky. "Lola, Mo, Lou, why don't you get your shoes on and a hoody. Who wants to take Angus to the river? I'll buy subs on the way from Lillie's and then just a quick trip to Co-op for groceries." She waits for the anti-grocery shopping argument, but they pause, turn, and go find their shoes.

"When did they get so *good*? Have they always been like this?"

Peter looks at her over the top of his banana but keeps chewing. On her way out of the kitchen Lola glances at the fat, white book on the counter.

"Who's Fabian Macomber? Wasn't that your dad's name? I didn't know he wrote a book." Bernie slides it off the counter.

"You wouldn't like it, too grown up." Lola pricks up. "I mean, too boring." Bernie walks to her bedroom and looks for a hiding place. Standing on tiptoe she makes room on her top shelf of the closet. The book falls open in her left hand and she almost drops the floppy weight. Glancing down she reads:

REVERSE PATRIARCHAL CHAOS The estab-. lished and dominating power of government, entertainment, advertising, secularized religion, institutional life in general is now *completely matriarchal*. It mechanically and obsessively reverses the patriarchal Nazi ideal of the militaristic father figure in command. Instead of 'Big Brother is watching you,' it's now 'Big Mother' in the 'back seat' driving. Not only is 'Big Mother' watching you, she's breathing down your neck, micromanaging your everyday life, guilt mongering, 'dick slapping', 'castrating', and force-feeding media and merchandise. The reverse-patriarchal 'monster' is hard at work feminizing male offspring with smothering, over-protective, hyper-attention. Her guilt-mongering methods and anti-male-attitudes . . .

Bernie throws the book across the room. It hits the wall and slides down, pages splayed. She stands vibrating. In a minute she walks over, picks it up again, and sits on the foot of the bed. She flips through, reading the headings:
Phoney and Dangerous Ethical Posturing
Macha Anti-intellectualism
The New Gatekeepers
How Hyper-feminism Institutionalizes Ingratitude
"Home Sweet Home"
Using Mass Immigration "Of Colour" Against the "Evil Aryan"

Bernie digs the base of her palms into her eye sockets. "Jesus Christ, what a . . . "

The bedroom door swings open and she looks up at Lou. He whirls a rubber-band ball the size of a walnut on its stretchy leash. Two more dangle from his pants pocket.

"We're ready Mom, I'm hungry, let's go get the subs. Can we eat them at the river?" Bernie's hand feels cold against her forehead and her temples throb.

"In a minute Lou, I'll come in a minute. Go out. Close the door."

Half an hour later Peter elbows his way through the back door. He holds his hands in front of him covered in chain lubricant. The three kids sit in front of the computer again, watching *Air Benders*.

"I thought you guys were going to the river. Where's your mom?"

Lola looks over her shoulder at him from her perch on the stool.

"She's in her room and she keeps saying she'll be out in a minute, but she seems kind of upset." In the bathroom Peter pumps soap into his hand and scrubs the grease from between his fingers. Down the hall he hears indistinct swearing, then a loud *thwack* as something dense hits the bedroom door. Peter flinches, rinses his hands and wipes them dry on his sweat pants. He opens the door.

"Bernie?" She paces around the room and looks up at him, her face wet and red. A little while later he walks back into the living room.

"Okay guys, I'm taking you to the river. Where's Angus?" The kids glance at him. "Come on, let's go. Who wants a milkshake?"

When they return, the driveway sits empty in the late afternoon sun. Peter plays a game of Monopoly with the little kids and gets Eben out of his room to rake the front lawn. There aren't that many leaves really, but any excuse to get the supine one upright. Later, before Peter goes to take a nap, he changes the password on the Apple to "mortise". Under "password hint" he writes "joint". Eben looks over his father's shoulder on his way to the kitchen.

"That's easy, I bet the password's 'doobie'."

"Ebe could you stay downstairs and keep an eye out for the kids, your mom's not back yet and I'm going to take a nap." Peter dials Bernie's cell number but hears her ringtone from the shelf in the front hall. In the basement he lies down on the couch in the family room.

In the early dusk Eben is detectable only by the white radiance of his cell phone screen, as he sits in the living room surfing YouTube videos. He contemplates texting Madison Harding about what she told him on the bus, but he doesn't know what to say.

Down the hall in Lola's bedroom Lou hunkers in the farthest corner on the floor. Opposite him a bull's eye drawn on the back of a shoebox balances on a pile of books. He pulls back on the rubber-band ball until it reaches his cheek and sights along his thumb, the tether strains. Release. *Whack*. The shoebox topples backwards, and he chuckles before going to the kitchen and digging around in the recycling bin. He comes back with three empty tin cans and some Yop bottles.

"Get out of my room, Lou! Why do you have to do that in here?"

107

"What?" says Lou. He arranges a new array of missile targets on top of the shoebox. If he hits even one of the Yop bottles, the strike will create a great domino effect.

Lola stands, bent over plastic vials illuminated in the circle of light from her desk lamp; the only other light in the room the low red glow of Cynthia's heat lamp. The hedgehog roots quietly in her wood-chip bedding. Lola drips lavender oil from a dropper into her mixture. Stirring, she consults the *Girl's Own Guide to Lovely Lotions*. Moira squirms on the tall stool, her shoulders wrapped in a towel, and a headband holding the curls off her face.

"Can't I go now? This 'nourishing' cream itches."

"First I have to try the detangler." Lola pours the mixture into a small squirt bottle and shakes. "Stay still now, close your eyes. Oh, here comes Mom, I wonder where she went. Close your eyes I said, I'm going to spritz." Outside the window the van sits idling. Their mother leans her forehead against her hands on the top of the steering wheel. Lou comes to look. "I wonder why she's just sitting there. Lou, go see why she's not coming in."

"Well if she's crying again, I don't want to . . . "

"Just sneak around to the side of the van, maybe she's listening to the radio." Lou decides he will go out the back door and scale the chain-link swing gate, just because it seems the stealthier thing to do. Dropping to the ground he bellies from bush to bush until he's huddled by the rear wheel of the minivan. After awhile he retreats the way he came.

"She's listening to Chris Smither, but that depressing song she usually skips, and she keeps hitting repeat." Lou sets up an array of Yop bottles on top of the book pile, sights again, and let's fly. The bungee-tailed missile goes

108

wide and ricochets off the corner of the bookcase. The ball smacks into the aluminum shade of Cynthia's heat lamp. The red glow snuffs out and Lola whirls.

"You broke her heat lamp! I told you not to do that in here. Where's dad? Dad!" she yells. Storming down the hall in the gloom she bumps into Eben.

"Dad's taking a nap. What are you yelling about? Is Mom back yet?"

"She's sitting in her car in the driveway. I think she's still crying. Lou bashed Cynthia's heat lamp. He broke the bulb!"

"There's some more in the broom closet. I'll go get one." In a minute he returns and unscrews Cynthia's bulb and inserts the new one. The cage glows amber. He looks out the window at his mother's van.

"Why is the light so yellow?"

"I don't know. Mom must have bought a different brand." They hear the front door open and watch Bernie walk past on her way to the bathroom. The faucet runs and the toilet flushes. She comes back and sticks her puffy face into the room.

"You guys all right? Where's Daddy? I'm sorry about the river and the afternoon. It's just, I'm trying . . . It's just some upsetting information about my father. I'm sorry. Did you eat?" They shake their heads. Bernie flips the wall switch. "I'll go cook something. Why doesn't anyone turn on lights?"

Opening the fridge, she realizes anew that she needed to buy groceries. In the pantry she finds four partial bags of pasta. A third of a block of aged but mouldy cheddar lies in the cheese drawer. She gets out some margarine and milk, flour from the cupboard, Dijon mustard.

Putting a pan of water on to boil she forgets to add the salt. The bags of pasta each have a different cooking time, ten minutes for the farfalle, eight for the penne, rotini thirteen, macaroni ten. While she makes the roux for the cheese sauce she calculates when each bag of pasta should be added to the water. She sets the timer for three minutes and puts in the rotini, when that goes off, she sets it for two . . .

"It's time to 'lock and load' with heavy duty intellectual ammunition."

Bernie throws in the penne. Stirs maniacally.

"His erotic addiction to the Hyper-Liberal 'white' woman may be 'Whitey's fatal Achilles heel." She chucks in the macaroni and the farfalle and sets the timer for eight.

"When we step back and think about it, the remarkably valuable Asian woman might be the best option for heterosexual Whitey." . . . The timer rings, she throws the whole mess into the colander in the sink. Bernie pares the mould off the cheese and then grates it into the pan of cream sauce. She tastes some from a spoon, pretty bland, not enough cheese so she adds a tablespoon of Dijon, what the hell, another one for Whitey.

Newspapers and felt pens, banana peels, a half-finished game of Monopoly cover the dining table, but she pushes the mess to the far end and lays out the bowls of mac and cheese and glasses of milk. She should go to the garden and see if any lettuce survived the frost, but darkness shrouds the yard.

"Come eat guys! Where's your dad?"

"Taking a nap Mommy," says Moira.

Sitting at the table, the children look down at their bowls then sideways at each other. Lola takes a tentative

110

bite of both mushy and too-chewy pasta and manages to swallow despite the odd stinging quality. Just then Peter comes up the stairs. He rubs his fists into his eye sockets.

"Man, did I ever fall asleep. How late is it? Eight o-clock all ready?" He looks carefully at Bernie's face. "Why don't you come into the bedroom and talk to me."

She gets up from the table.

"I'll be back in a little while to read to you guys."

"That's okay," says Lola. "We don't need a story tonight. We'll just go to sleep."

"Don't worry about the dishes," says Eben.

When they hear the bedroom door close, they go dig in the fridge for something edible but come out empty handed.

"Daddy bought groceries, but why does he think we all have to be on his Keto diet?" wails Lola. "There's nothing but yogurt and cheese and nuts and kale!"

"Don't ask Dad for food, he'll just make you another green smoothie, says Eben, but then he remembers the Ichiban under his bed.

"Lola unloads, Lou and Mo load. I'll make Ichiban," he says before heading up the stairs to get it.

"Try again."

Fabian stares at the screen and forces himself to think "other", to imagine what the blood-sucking vacuum of need could possibly want now. Again, he visualizes himself defenseless and immobile, exposed and cold, and the screen clears a spot in the opalescence like a hair dryer melting a frosty window.

"Oh! Oh! Keep the focus! Excellent." Through the aperture the egg uncurls and flails. *Warm*, thinks Fabian. *Contain me.* Baby David seems to relax into his skin and settle into expectant waiting. *Suck. Suck a lot.* The baby burps but stares through the screen disgruntled. *Good Lord suck some more then.* Fabian scores a smile. *Always come, always come when I shout*, and finally he responds with a fast forward spurt of maturation. In a blink he grows from an off-kilter baby, to a sitting upright Buddha, robust and complacent.

"Wow! Very good, you've grown him to six months. Now what do you see? What does he need?"

Fabian sighs and hugs his knees to his chest as he sits. He stares at baby David, what did he Fabian want at this point? *Eyes, watch me, watch me.* Mirror, adore. *Smiles, hands there, contain but let me go too.* Touch me! The infant morphs again. Suddenly Fabian cannot watch, he rotates away with a jerk and the screen gives off a squawk like the needle dragged across a vinyl record.

"Always the babies! The bloody babies! How can I give what I never received? I never got *touch*, or *mirror*, or *adore!*" and yet I must provide ceaselessly?" He stands, walks away from the screen and paces. "Finally, with Margaret I thought I would get my share. She oozed maternity. Finally, I would have nurturing and companionship and *sex!* But David came the first year we were married. He hypnotized her. He sucked up my entire cut. He made her hate me."

"The baby and mother do hypnotize each other. They can't help it. You must admire and encourage this dance, an exhausting and virtuous infatuation . . . "

112

"Moronic prancing around the diaper pail, more like it," finishes Fabian. "Any intellectual rigour she contained turned to mush, and the whole process, the swelling and birthing, ugh, disgusting. They stretched out her lovely skin. She squandered her beauty on them instead of saving it for me."

Bune stares at the cantankerous toddler for a long time and scratches his head.

"To be honest with you I'm not sure how to proceed."

"With what? My *indoctrination?*"

"I can't seem to find any crack in your armour." Again, Bune materializes a cigarette. He paces slowly into the dark trailed by regular puffs of smoke.

"Where are you going?"

"Just walking for awhile."

"Walking where? That's the way to the Sponsor Ring, are you going to go visit? What's it like? I wonder if . . . " Bune stops just before vanishing from sight in the black. The puffs of smoke slow. Deliberately he rotates. The two extra heads erupt from his shoulders, and all take on expressions of benign affability as he walks back.

"Logically speaking," says the wolf head gruffly, "by the law of cause and effect, 'karma' if you will, any insight you achieve here on Corridor Nine will be immediately rewarded."

"An essential characteristic, a biological function perhaps," continues Bune's angel head.

"Will be restored to you," the griffin rasps, tilting his head sideways to fix his beady eye on Fabian. "For instance, because of your marginally successful completion of Lesson One you regained the capacity for physical exhaustion, as you recall." He fidgets the ridged edges of his beak together gently.

"But alternatively," concludes Bune "other rewards are up for negotiation." Fabian straightens, hands clasped behind his back and ponders the three-headed being.

"What are you suggesting?"

"Other recompenses perhaps. For instance, a field trip of some sort . . . "

"You mean to the Sponsor Ring?"

"Yes. An orientation, so you can plan your next assignment and to provide motivation for your last two lessons."

"Absolutely!" cries Fabian. "That seems fair, absolutely. Count me in!"

"All right, then. Let's do a lap and then get back to work. Do you want to pick the form I will assume for our walk? Variety will refresh us both." Fabian wags his pink finger from head to head.

"Eeny meany miney mo. I pick the dog." In a moment the wolf rubs his head against Fabian's shoulder and they set out.

⊶⊷⊶

Bernie stands on the stepladder and reaches to the top of the wall of books, slides her hand into the hole left by the copy Peter had brought home, and gets her fingers under the next identical book behind it. David wants one, and she will wrap and send it to him before she picks the kids up from school. She tugs and wiggles the massive paperback out of the misaligned front layer and stops. Her headlamp shines into the hole and on tiptoe she can just see the back surface of the cavity. A wide crack oozes

114

hardened Bulldog adhesive, a glimpse of a two-by-four between the gypsum panels.

"Oh my God!" She starts pulling books from the top of the stack, widening the hole and throwing them behind her until she gets that section of wall down to chest height. "When will I get to the end of this?" She slides her hand back in against the wall and pulls with all her force, managing to tip the balance and the books domino down around her almost knocking over the stepladder. Too late, Bernie realizes she buried the sledgehammer and spends five minutes digging to unearth it. Stepping wobbly back across the new higher ground, she looks, and his writing greets her. This time just one word.

PSYCHEDELIA

Drawn to the right of the "A" stands one of his cartoons, sketched in a few quick strokes as if seen from behind, a mouse complete with rectum dot, tail draped over arm, head sideways to show snout and whiskers. His other hand holds a valise and he walks away from Bernie, stepping into new and festive territory. She gets out her cell phone, turns on the flash, and takes a picture. Here stands the mouse in the last scene of the little book *Francis the House Mouse*. He wrote it for her and David when they were small. A few years ago, she finally burnt it in the fireplace. *Francis is a house mouse. Oh, where is his house? Where is a mouse to go? Francis doesn't know. Everywhere mice wonder too.*

The basement seems drained of air. Bernie wishes she'd brought Angus. She picks up David's copy and struggles over the books and up the stairs.

⊹⊹⊹

"Can't we repair him?"

"Mmmm. Sorry, no rewind function I'm afraid." The toddler seems oddly caved in, with the disfiguring indentation running under his chest, up his throat, and settling in the uncertainty of his eyes.

"Well, it looks very much like him actually, the expression at any rate. That's why he always seemed . . . ?" Fabian looks up at the wolf.

"Yes."

Fabian turns away, wraps his arms around the thick ruff of the dog's neck, and talks into the muffling fur.

"Jealousy overcame me you see, when he took more and more of her. He became a wedge between us. I mean my jealousy was, was the wedge. But you can't understand the power of the feeling, like a wave, a tidal wave. I fought it. I felt shame, but the envy knocked me down, swept me away, so far out that what was the point in coming back to see what I had done?" Fabian seems to shake and Bune pulls away so he can see him. With his long tongue he licks the contorted face.

"If you'd like I could return your tears now. After I'd given up all hope, I do believe you completed Lesson Two." Fabian breathes a long sigh; he rolls around to sit, leaning back against the wolf's hip.

"I miss tears, but I thought you said the reward was negotiable? Have I really completed Lesson Two?"

"We will practise some more with the girl egg. But essentially yes, and of course, the field trip, if you prefer. Let's pack him up now. If you like you could apologize to him. That usually helps everyone."

Fabian stares through the screen at David. *It's not your fault. My fault. So sorry.* Very slowly the indentation pushes

116

out, settling on the toddler's skin a long and puckered scar.

"His eyes look happier, don't you think?" asks Fabian.

"Yes. Too wise for a three-year-old, but happier. You are right. Now just say goodbye."

"Will he feel this, do you think? The grown-up man in the real world, will this change how *he* feels too?"

"Yes, at an unconscious level he heard your apology."

Goodbye and best wishes, thinks Fabian, suddenly shy. The wolf walks to the corner of the screen and looks quizzically at him. Fabian nods. Bune curls back his lips, delicately pinches the tail end of the rip strip with his teeth and pulls.

⊕⊕⊕

Bernie jumps. In the sun, curled against the arm of the settee, a puddle of charcoal fur lifts its head.

"Smokey?" His eyes are greener than the mossy velvet but his fur retreats in places, forgetting how to grow. The cat yawns wide, showing all the teeth, his black gorge, a pink and freckled tongue. He pushes up stiffly to sit, and half-hobbles half-pours himself onto the floor.

"Mrwow." She thinks he must be eighteen now. The world's most ancient cat and her father's only successful relationship. She crouches as he circles, rubbing his forehead and cheeks against her knees, his boney ribs vibrating like an old Model T. Bernie scratches under his new rhinestone-studded collar then works her fingers down his back and gives him an especially good scratch at the base of the tail.

"Nice collar. Looks like Mrs. Gotslieg treats you right. How'd you get in?" He follows her, rubbing around her ankles as she walks from room to room.

Oh, she forgot to close the bathroom window. Bernie pulls it shut and goes back to the living room, empty except for the settee. It waits, poised on its curved legs, eagle feet gripping cherry-wood spheres. She sits and lifts Smokey beside her, then spreads the manifesto on her knees. David wants a sample, so Bernadette takes pictures with her cell phone and attaches them to texts. She sends the pages:

"How nazis and hyper-liberals use double standards to override ethical obiligations, Whitey's reward, Drawing and quartering the heterosexual white male."

Bernie kneels and takes a picture of the cat in the sun and sends that to David too. Her phone rings.

"Hey Bern."

"David! I thought you'd be working."

"I'm good. Just finishing some charting and my last patient cancelled. Quite the book eh? But I think you're taking it too personally, I mean . . . "

"Everything I am David, *everything I am* he hated. He despised in fact. Women *educated* white women, mothers. Especially mothers. And, David, before *anything else, I am a mother.*"

"I know, but he probably wasn't thinking about you, maybe you were an exception in his mind."

"I don't think so. Remember the "Secret Santa" packages on Christmas morning?"

"Oh right, didn't he lower them with a pulley and rope from the neighbour's tree?"

"Yes, and they were entirely *full* of toy guns, like fifty per box. Clearly, he thought I was a hyper-liberal, castrating mother. Even Eben, and he was only five, said; 'I didn't think Santa liked guns *that* much.'"

"That's when you moved."

"Yes, the last straw in a long string of weird shit. To address unknown."

"Well, way back, Bernie, I had to make the decision to stop caring or go crazy. If it makes you feel any better, this obsessive paranoid thinking is typical of long-term drug use. He just keeps repeating himself and going in circles in this book. I've seen it before. Totally crazy, but clever in a lot of places though, don't you think?"

"Yeah. It's a shame."

"Are you going to break through the Psychedelia wall now? Maybe you should wait for Peter to come with you." Bernie rubs her forehead.

"You know, I just want to get to the end of this. I'm fine. Hey, I've got Smokey here for company. What a great old cat."

"Okay. Well give him a scratch from me and send photos of the next chamber."

"I will." She stands up, puts the phone in her vest pocket and pulls the headlamp back on. "You stay here cat. Wait until I've finished the demolition."

The drywall crumples at the weight of the hammer. Bernie smashes with abandon, but she stops short of Francis the House Mouse. Stepping in, the colour momentarily dazzles after all the white books. This room is bigger, twelve feet to the next wall and plastered with brilliant posters. The headlamp picks out a periwinkle blue eye, the iris worked in intricate whorls and arabesques of turquoise. Beside it a magenta pink print, covered in the same complex organic forms but in black, and more diffuse; like patterns of gasoline on a puddle or the trailing smoke of a Chinese dragon. Her father's "acid prints", his silkscreens. Spinning, she realizes he tried to cover all four walls until he ran out of prints. Most are mandalas, sometimes framed in kaleidoscopic, diagonally stretched checkerboard patterns. Always the intricate pen and ink squiggles fill in the outlines but in every saturated hue. Mexican pink, chartreuse, egg yolk, carnelian, moss, azure, persimmon. Bernie reads the titles in the corners, Mandala 12, Cerebral Cosmograph, Cosmograph 5. She stands again in his garage studio just able to see over his worktable, feels the heat of the white blazing spot lights, the void behind Fabian's eyes as he works for hours with dip pen and India ink. Rolling Stones and Bob Dylan and Mozart blast from the stereo. "Daddy?" she hears her little voice, but when he got like that there was no point talking to him. At a later session he'd photoprint the drawings onto their silkscreens, still later squeegee the brilliant inks across the surface for multiple prints. Sometimes he'd talk to her then, as the more manual labour didn't require the inspiration of LSD.

Her phone gives off its canned impression of a camera shutter, *ka-sha, ka-sha, ka-sha.* These signify how many hours of acid-tripping have curdled his brains. Towards one wall sits her cookstove, made from a small wooden filing cabinet, red light bulb burners that really turned on under a white Plexiglas top. The doll cradle. The rocking boat takes up a quarter of the space. Six blue plastic storage boxes sit stacked in a corner. She lifts the first one and starts lugging it out through the ragged drywall fissures and over the unpredictable footing of the books. Bernie finally makes it to the stairs and looks up to Smokey's silhouette in the mouth of the doorway.

"Mrwow?"

"I'm coming."

When she opens it on the splintery hardwood of the living room, the box erupts with black and white photographs. *Time Life* quality, exhaustive documentation of her bohemian childhood. The sound of the shutter and the big black eye of the lens, her father's most consistent attributes, and she and David his constant subjects. With sinking heart she sorts through them, David runs, a milkweed stalk aloft to the wind. The two of them and Randy and Sally Gotslieg in the plywood rocking boat under the poplars. A naked toddler Bernie crouches to pick up apples, her fuzzy orangutan outline caressed by the sun. Birthday cakes, Easter egg decorating, dress-up, dogs and cats and pet rabbits, paint and art and nature.

Look, look, look what we gave you. Behind her right shoulder her father vibrates outraged indignation. Here David runs parallel with the surf on Long Beach dragging a whiplash of kelp. The Cabin in Nelson, the chicken coop and Indian sweat lodge. Bernie and David taking a bath at sundown in a claw foot tub floating in a field of daisies.

Look what we gave you!

But see our eyes? It wasn't always so pretty. She picks up a group shot of their family and friends in front of a derelict barn. The baby-faced wives with their poetic hair gaze at husbands in groovy beards, funky felt hats, and intellectual black-rimmed glasses. The children showcase avant-garde charm.

Idiots, innocents, thinks Bernie, and Fabian splutters, *We were skewering convention to the heart of the truth!*

No. You were just blowing your mind. In the cathedral of a fir tree, Bernie peeks around a branch. Bernie and David stand balanced on a log in Kootenay Lake, suntanned and free.

Argue with that.

But you chose the pictures.

She hasn't eaten breakfast and now it's past lunch, but she can't think of food. The cat sleeps on the couch and Bernie sits with her face in her hands. A knock at the kitchen door makes her jump.

"Who on earth? Oh." Through the window in the kitchen door, a beehive of grey curls. She opens it and there stands Eva Gotslieg, softer, wider in the hip and lower in the bust, the chestnut curls now silver. But the same drooping owl-eye glasses, the same gimlet glint and fierce sociability.

"Oh! Hello Eva! How are you? I'm so sorry I haven't dropped by before, it's been . . . "

"Don't be silly, dear. I didn't expect you to. I thought you could use a cup of coffee and a bite to eat, so I brought some of my plum cake. I'm a bit worried though; I can't find your father's cat. He wouldn't happen . . . "

"Ah, Smokey! Come in here." She leads the way to the living room where Smokey reclines comatose. "I left the bathroom window open last time, and he must have climbed in."

"That's a relief. A coyote would make quick work of him." Mrs. Gotslieg sits on the settee beside him and puts her grocery tote on the floor, extracts from it two plastic Tim Horton's go-cups and hands one to Bernie. "Come sit. I hope you don't take sugar. I just put in a little cream." Bernie sits and glances sideways at Eva's lavender sweatshirt where two chickadees cavort on a branch strained across the bust. A modest crucifix lies centreed between the points of the pink polo collar. Mrs. Gotslieg looks at the black and white photos strewn on the floor.

"So how are Susie and Randy? I think about them a lot. Is Randy in the fire department still?"

"Oh, they're fine, just fine. They both live in Calgary now, so I see them often. Randy actually went back to school and got a degree in social work. He has a wife and two little girls. My pride and joy, and Susie nurses now, she has a nice boyfriend and works at the Foothills in intensive care."

"That's wonderful that they're so close, that you're so close."

"Well, I always told them 'Sticking with family is what makes it family'."

Bernie looks down at her feet and feels the blood creep away from her face and chest to some unspecified destination. She looks up. The neighbour leans forward and stares with intensity into her face.

"What I meant to say was 'Family means no one gets left behind or forgotten'." Bernie's blood decides to abandon ship altogether, it trickles as far away as possible, in this case due south to her feet. The crucifix glares at her.

"'Honour thy father and mother'," Bernie says huskily. She tightens her hands around the plastic cup. The neighbour reaches out and touches her knee.

123

"I think you misunderstand me, dear. Do you know the other half to that? What is it? Ah, Ephesians 6, I think. 'Honour thy father and mother that it may go well with you and you may live long in the land.' But people don't often know about the second half of the verse. It reads something like 'Fathers do not embitter your children, lest they become discouraged.'"

Her vision suddenly murky, Bernie gawps into the beam of the owl-eyed glasses. The muscles of her face quiver just out of control, Eva keeps talking.

"Your father forgot David, didn't he? Left him behind, and in a different way he forgot you too. My Leonard used to say, 'nice people, but something's not right in that house'."

Bernie gives up as the hot wet slides down her face. Eva Gotslieg holds her hand and gives her a napkin.

"I sometimes think," Bernie hauls herself back from the brink, mops her face. "I sometimes think if I had stayed in touch, maybe I could have convinced him to go to rehab." She blows her nose.

"Two good women spent a lot of time trying to fix your dad. Your mother of course, and Serena finally left, you know, because he refused treatment. I doubt you'd have had any more leverage."

Bernie takes a sip of the coffee. It slips down her gullet, creamy and hot, relaxing the knots on the way. She drinks again. From a Tupperware box Eva hands her a plastic fork and a square of cake on a napkin. Bernie bites, dense, mildly sweet with the autumnal tang of plums.

"This is very good," Bernie mumbles through the crunchy cinnamon crumbs, waving her fork.

"My mother's recipe. I'll write it out for you. Besides, he was the father and you were the *child*. It was up to him not you."

After they finish the coffee, they talk about all the childhood adventures with Susie and Randy and David. Before Eva leaves, Bernie takes her to the basement and shows her the books and the bizarre partitions.

"Do you know when he built all this?" They stand surrounded by the acid prints. Eva goes to the rocking boat and pushes to set it going.

"Oh my. I remember all of you out playing in the yard on this, rocking it to high heaven." She looks around her and shakes her head. "Let me think. After his second operation maybe, when he was quite recovered. I saw more of him for a time. Yes! I watched him carry two-by-fours into the house, and Totem delivered some drywall. He said he was renovating the basement."

Bernie laughs.

They turn to leave and Bernie helps her neighbour scramble over all the books, and they go up the stairs.

"You said he had an operation?"

"Two, dear. He went to the Foothills for the second time, about a year-and-a-half ago. Something about a blockage in his bowels, I think? He said it was only a temporary measure, that he had chronic issues. Oh yes, 'It will be the end of me,' that's what he said. I didn't want to pry. He seemed embarrassed."

"That explains it then. In his suicide note he said something about a 'fatal disease'. I guess that's what he meant."

An hour later she closes the door behind Eva, gripping Smokey firmly against her bosom. Bernie watches them walk back to the white bungalow streaked with the shadow of poplar trees. In the living room she gathers up the photos off the floor and lays them in the storage box. Then she finds her headlamp and goes down to the basement.

First, she uncovers the wall, pulling out the pushpins and stacking up the posters on her baby cookstove. Towards the middle she finds the last word written in Sharpie: ANCESTORS.

The hammer makes quick work of it, and stepping in, her headlamp finally finds the far foundation of cemented river rock. Four more blue plastic storage boxes lie on the floor. She opens them and sees bundles of old letters in her grandma Evelyn's tiny writing, yellowed newspaper clippings, some war medals, a stiff sawdust-stuffed teddy bear, and stacks and stacks of sepia-toned photographs, mainly of Fabian at different ages and her grandparents. I can sort through these at home, she thinks. She picks up a storage box and starts hauling it to the van.

Bernie almost trips on the toy stove on her way out. She sets the bin down and looks at it, flips the switches that used to turn on the red light-bulb burners. Inside the drawer she finds the plastic dishes, white with sprigs of blue flowers. They are dirty with the remnants of some concoction, crushed flower petals, mud. Maybe Jell-O or Kool-Aid crystals have glued a stack of teacups together. She remembers her father giving it its final coat of harvest gold paint. Maybe she should bring it home for the twins and repaint it. She looks inside the oven and finds the enamel teapot her mother bought in Chinatown. David rushing around in the kitchen making tea for her parents, while Bernie listens to them yelling at each other in the living room. She closes the little oven door. I'll build them a new one, she thinks.

Fabian stirs from sleep to the occasional static crackle of the Membrane and the steady breath of Bune. He drifts out again into the eddy of his dream. Margaret lies warm against him. Her hair smells of Johnson's Baby Shampoo, the yellow kind that says "no more tears." He listens to the chirping of the children down the hall. He will capture all their dancing moments with his big black Nikon. The day stretches before him free of the usual muttering discontent, and he wants to leap to it, like a frog to a pool. He smiles as he hangs the Nikon on a branch by its strap. The branch is grey with lichen, but sturdy, and forms a hook. He touches the water with his toes, and then steps in to join David and Bernie. He feels the cool bracelets creeping up his ankles as he moves into the transparent green. I am here, I am here he says, squatting down, and selects for each of them the perfect water-silky pebble from the thousands on the bottom. He is surprised to see calm expectancy in his children's eyes, to feel a member of a tribe. Someone pushes on his back. Move along. But Fabian ignores the intrusion. Into David's hand he nests the flattened oval of jade and red oxide, divided with a seam of white quartz. Stop pushing! I'm not done yet. For Bernie this buffed-amber sea-glass lozenge. A chip off the end shows the congealed transparency inside the sandblasted skin. Just in time, he slides it into the cup of her palm then he turns around to see.

"I'm not done yet," snaps Fabian.

"Wake up tadpole. See how far the sun has risen. Today we will go on the field trip. You must eat."

"I'm not . . . " but the grey ceiling blots up his dream. He punches the turf. It forms around his knuckles, then extrudes him back out.

Fabian sits cross-legged and glowers up at Bune standing above him in full-angel format. The cloud gown and creamy feathers contrast with his calloused skin. Quickly Fabian reaches down and touches the angel's foot. Under the roughness it feels warm.

"Today an extra special breakfast," says Bune.

"Why?"

"It's Sunday. You have worked hard, made progress, and we will visit the Sponsor Ring, as I promised."

"The Sponsor Ring, where you go to select your next lifetime, your next assignment."

"That's right. Where you choose your sponsor. Not today of course. Today we will just get the lay of the land."

"By sponsor you mean my next mother? And by mother you also mean the Gateway?"

"Mmm, hmm. You are full of questions this morning. Now lie down and eat your breakfast so we can get going."

Fabian flops sideways and nestles into the turf.

"Why can't we have this on Earth? It's really such an excellent system, so efficient. No dishes, no grocery shopping, no chopping or stewing or grinding or baking, no refrigeration required. No botulism, no E. coli poisoning. You don't even have to brush your teeth!"

"Stop talking and eat."

He breathes for a while and breakfast arrives. Little round waffles, made with nut flour perhaps? Light and crisp, yet chewy. Dense, silky whipping cream. Tumbling

128

wild blue berries, golden currants, *fraise de bois*. For the carnivore, a hearty side of fried ham, texture perfect, no gristly bits. Fabian sits up and burps.

"You know, there was just one thing missing."

"Good Lord, lie down then."

He lies down. A big cup of kickass French roast. A deep sigh and Fabian smiles blissfully.

"Stand. Now rotate ninety degrees away from the Membrane. We are pointed due black you see? Now we walk."

"How far do we have to walk? Is it further than one 'circumnavigation of the lifetimes of man'?"

"Twice the distance actually. I regret restoring your capacity for exhaustion; we may need to rest." Bune extends his nomad foot, the cloud gown murmurs of rain and Fabian falls into a dogtrot beside him. For a while they walk in silence, the light receding until they are engulfed in dark. A vacuum surrounds them. Fabian can detect nothing beyond his own childish pant and the soft rasp of the angel's calloused feet against the nap of the turf.

"How will we know if we're walking straight? I mean what if we veer off and just wander around in circles?"

"Well if you are worried you can hold my hand."

"But how do *you* know? How do you not get off track?"

"I just feel my way." Bune stops, reaches out in the dark and finds Fabian's shoulder. "As always the turf predicts our needs. Kneel." Fabian drops to all fours and runs his paws over the carpet.

"Oh!" Under his hands the softness organizes itself into rows running away from him. "It feels like corduroy!"

"Yes, follow the grain and you can't get lost. Shall we proceed?" Fabian stands up and again starts to trot but he doesn't get through more than twenty of Bune's paces before the density of the blackness overwhelms him. He feels his puny bit of self in danger of snuffing out. He begins to hyperventilate. Blindly he claws until he touches Bune and finds the calloused hand.

"Sensory deprivation getting to you?"

"It's so endless, and thick, I feel like I'm going to dissolve, like I'll get sucked away."

"The next time we go you won't mind so much, once you know where the end is. But maybe we should talk, or I know, did you used to sing?"

"Very badly. Couldn't do sports, sang offkey, and danced like Mr. Bean. The whole prowess area, beyond my intellectual capacities was a fiasco. I used to put marbles up my nose to imitate Bob Dylan though. Actually, I did a passable Bob Dylan. Margaret could stay on key, but not me."

"Well pick a Bob Dylan song then. What was your favourite?"

"Oh, there were so many. Let me think. How about 'A Hard Rain's Gonna Fall'? Do you know that one?"

"I can generally catch the gist. You start, and I'll back you up. Ready, and we'll walk." Fabian aligns his toes in the ribs of turf, and grips Bune's finger. He opens his mouth and the first words quaver out, the mother's question to her son.

"Deep breath and a little louder," says Bune.

Fabian launches back in, reiterating the question.

"Now it's coming! Belt it out! On Corridor Nine you can sing like you never dreamed."

130

With gusto, Fabian chews into the gritty lament. Bune stops and turns to him in the dark.

"Really? Are you sure that's the sound you want? It sounds like, like . . . "

"It sounds like sandpaper singing! That was Bob Dylan! Wow, it's just like him, even without the marbles up my nose. How will you catch on if you don't know the lyrics?"

"I've 'tuned into your wavelength'. You sing sandpaper, and I'll back you up with bass."

Fabian howls out the next line.

"Now you come in with your part," and Bune's low roll of thunder joins the little guy's nasal trumpet call.

Fabian closes his eyes, so they can stop straining against the dark. He feels the lines of turf falling away behind each searching step — foothills undulating, the scudding shadows of cloud tangling with sunlight. Far ahead he can make out the indigo line of the mountains.

⟲⟳⟲

Eben scrubs out the mac and cheese saucepan, while Lola loads the last of the dishes into the dishwasher. The twins sit on opposite sides of the banquette. Lola found them a bag of potato chips in the back of the snack cupboard, and they nosh steadily while they wait for the kettle to boil for the Ichiban.

"Has she always been like this? I mean, what did it used to be like?" asks Lola, straightening up and pushing the dishwasher door with her hip until it grinds shut. "It's hard to remember."

"Who? Mom?"

"Yeah."

131

"I'm thirsty," pipes Louis. "Can I have some of Daddy's Starbucks cold brew?"

Eben picks the litre bottle up from the counter and unscrews the cap, sucks back a mouthful and thinks.

"No cold brew. You're too young for that much caffeine. Have some milk, there's protein and calcium in milk. 'Always have protein with your carbs'." He steps to the fridge and takes out the carton, waggles it at Lola. "She'd be around all the time, saying stuff like that, you know useful rules to live by." He pulls two plastic kid cups out of the cupboard.

"We're watching way too much media now. 'Turn off the computer!' She said *that* constantly." Lola gets herself a cup too. "What else?" turning to the twins.

"'Boredom is just creativity warming up,'" says Moira

"'Wait five days, and if you still want it go back and buy it,'" continues Louis. "She just says that because she knows I'll forget. Hey wait a minute! I never got that dagger letter opener from the Egyptian store."

"We used to go places," says Moira. "It's boiling, Eben." He peels the plastic tops half open on the Styrofoam Ichiban cups and fills each one from the kettle, then sets the timer on the microwave for two minutes.

"We used to have projects, or she'd get all excited about something. Remember Mexican cooking and masa harina, home-made tortillas?"

"The summer when we got the potter's wheel," says Louis.

"Paper making!"

"Candles, that whole beeswax phase."

"The year she built the tree house, and we helped her," says Lola.

132

"Well we didn't help too much, I snuck into the house when we were working on the post holes for the foundation. She finished them herself with a shovel and her soup ladle." Eben picks up the Coke bottle and takes another swig. "God, and the yoga, when she made us all do yoga. We were so little." He gets four spoons and pulls the lids all the way off the Ichiban cups, puts one in front of each twin. "But it was fun actually, and I still do it you know, sometimes when I can't sleep. You guys eat that and then go to bed, it's school tomorrow." He and Lola lean against the kitchen counter and eat standing up.

"We used to just talk a lot. Tell her about stuff. Now she just says 'aha' and 'mmm'. You know I wish I had met her dad. What was his name?"

"Fabian."

"What a weird name. You saw him a few times, didn't you? There's that picture in your baby book, when he came to the hospital after you were born."

"He used to stop by the little house sometimes, this short bald guy with big black glasses. He wouldn't ever look at me, but he brought me a gift once, an easel for painting. I think he made it himself out of plywood, but it was so heavy, and the hinges didn't lock. It fell over one day and scraped my leg. After that she must have thrown it out and we got that cheap easel from IKEA."

"And you were there weren't you, for the 'Secret Santa Package'?"

"Oh yeah!" says Eben. "You were just a baby. I remember looking out the patio doors, you know to the back deck we had in the little house? It was snowing."

"Was it Christmas morning?"

"Yes, I think we'd opened gifts and were getting ready for breakfast. This huge present wrapped in red and gold paper with a big red ribbon, it looked like a Christmas decoration at the Bay. It came out of the sky very slowly in little jerks and landed on the deck. *Whump!* The snow flew up all around it. It was as big as a dishwasher!"

"How did he do that?"

"Well then I saw him up in the neighbour's tree, looking at me through those glasses. He'd lowered it by a rope and I guess he didn't want to come down and untie it. The rope landed on the deck like a snake. I looked up again, and he was gone."

"And it was full of toy guns, right?" asks Lola.

"Yeah, totally full. I've never seen so many, oh and a tin frog that you could wind up with a key. Mom said I could only pick out two guns to keep, and the frog."

"I want a story, will she come out in time for stories?" Moira fishes out the last of the instant noodles and drinks the salty broth out of the bottom of the cup.

Lola looks at Eben. "I'll go check'" she says and walks down the hall. She stands for a minute looking at the crack of light under her mother's bedroom door, and then goes back to the kitchen.

"They're talking, and I think she's crying again. I'll tuck you in and give you a back rub okay?"

"I want Momma." Louis scratches at the tops of his hands, his neck. "I feel all itchy."

"He's getting that rash, Eben."

"Come on Lou, the calamine's in your room." Eben steers his little brother by the top of the head out of the kitchen with the girls following. In the bottom bunk he pulls off Louis' shirt and examines his back and chest.

134

"Well it's still just his hands and his neck. Do you think it will affect his breathing?" he asks Lola.

"I don't know."

He squirts the pink calamine lotion into his palm, rubs his hands together and then applies it to his squirming little brother.

"That tickles, it's cold!"

"Shut up, do you want to itch or not?" He turns to Lola. "I've got to study for my science test, I'll come check on his breathing before I go to sleep."

"Okay," says Lola. "I'll give them a back rub."

"But I want stories!" Moira insists from the top bunk.

"No time, I have to clean Cynthia's cage. Did you guys brush your teeth? Go brush your teeth and I'll give you a quick back rub, hurry up."

An hour later Bernie splashes cold water on her face and wonders why crying makes her feel so exhausted, blown out from the inside. Her eyes ache. Behind her, Peter soaps his hair in the shower. She looks at her watch. It says ten fifteen.

"Oh my God, the kids!" Quickly she dries her face and opens the bedroom door. Dark and quiet fill the house. Angus sits at the back door. He paws it mechanically like he's been doing every thirty seconds for the last half hour. She lets him out for the final pee of the night.

By the glow of the night light she sees Louis' freckled face lying sideways on his pillow, his eyelids twitch and a rivulet of expression flickers over his face so fast she can't catch the story line. He ends with a watery grin and nuzzles his cheek deeper into the pillow. Bernie climbs the ladder to check on Moira who lies curled in fetal position. She can't see her face, but she touches the gold fuzz of her hair for a moment and climbs back down.

No light shines under Lola's door further down the hall, and Bernie doesn't want to risk its grating against the floor when it opens. Something must be wrong with the hinges, maybe the screws have worn their way out of the wood with kids swinging on it. She needs to buy longer thicker screws at Totem, but she keeps forgetting. Looking up, yellow light spills onto the landing from Eben's room. Slowly she climbs the stairs. He sits hunched over his desk, textbooks spread around him, his earbuds in and the lines running to the pocket of his hoodie. She watches for a moment, how the raw bones in his face have lengthened. The acne on his cheekbones looks painful and inflamed. Sensing something, he turns to her and jumps.

"Sorry. I surprised you. Did you put everyone to bed? Thank you, you shouldn't have to. Things will be better soon; I'm almost on top of . . . " She stops, remembering how many times she's said this. Eben thinks of Louis' rash while he takes in his mother's puffy features and swollen red eyes, how her shoulders cave forward.

"It's okay," he says. "They listened pretty well. I don't mind."

"Why are you still working?"

"I have a science test tomorrow."

"Are you almost done? Don't stay up too much longer, okay? Better to sleep. If you're too tired you can't remember anything anyhow."

"I won't be long."

"And Eben,"

"Yeah?"

136

"Thanks buddy." She turns, and he listens to her go back down the stairs. He reaches into his pocket and takes out his phone. He sets his alarm for one o'clock to check on Louis again, then for six forty-five so he'll be up early enough to catch the school bus. The bus. He should talk to Madison. He can't avoid this forever, but he really doesn't know what to tell her.

⟜⟐⟜⟐⟜⟐

"How much further?"

"One third to go. Do you want to rest or eat something?"

"No, let's just get there. How many more songs is 'one third to go'?"

"If they are Bob Dylan songs, I imagine only three or four, but please, didn't you sing anything else?"

"But he wrote so many and I can remember the lyrics perfectly here. This is a great one; actually you have a choice. Do you want 'It's All Right Ma I'm Only Bleeding' or 'Tangled Up in Blue'?"

"Oh God help me, sounds like more of the same. 'Tangled Up In Blue', I guess, but then, please can we move onto a different artist, a different genre perhaps?"

"Well Margaret and I used to sing folk songs with the kids, though they lack the penetrating vision of Bob Dylan. Oh! I know! Leadbelly, I'd love to sing like Leadbelly, but first 'Tangled Up in Blue'," and he launches in with gusto.

"You sing too, come on." Bune sighs and his baritone rumbles in to join Fabian.

⟜⟐⟜⟐⟜⟐

Bernie pulls into her driveway after dropping the kids off for school. Angus sits sentinel in the passenger seat. The

137

blue storage bins wait in the back of the van. She decides to take them to her studio and look at the photos there. First, she puts the dog in the house, and then she carries each bin to the swing gate. She sets the numbers on the combination lock and unlatches it, pushes the gate open and drags the boxes into the backyard.

The wind gusts and dislodges the last red leaves from the crabapple tree. They flare against the grey sky before circling down to the lawn. Across the yard the studio hunkers in the naked grove of aspen, its windows dark. The weather vane on the roof rotates with a squawk. Bernie looks up at it as she puts the box down. Why does she keep it? She should just get a ladder and take it down. The sun and moon cut from a sheet of tin while little Bernie sits cross-legged on her dad's worktable to watch. She twists the door handle and pushes it open, bends over and drags in the first box.

Her studio is so jam-packed with old bikes, garden tools, and camping gear that there is nowhere to put the box down. Today she will make room and clear this junk out. Leaving the box on a pile of winter tires, Bernie picks up two rolls of garden hose and slings them over a shoulder, grabs a rake, two trowels, some loppers, and clamps a folded green tarp under her arm. They can all go in the garden shed. She sees the twins' bikes from two years ago. Those she can donate, and the four other bikes can be stored in the garage.

Two hours later, after a trip to Cycle Rama and dumping boxes of kitchenware and old skates at the Women in Need, Bernie stares at the little room, light filtering through the dirty window, empty except for the camping gear piled neatly against one wall. She walks to the kitchen to get a broom and fills a bucket with soapy water. Soon the red-painted plywood floor, the counter, and sink are clean. She scours the big multipaned window with vinegar water and a microfiber cloth, then drags her easel back into place and sets it up. One of the two aluminum-shaded spotlights still have a functional bulb, but she switches it off, preferring the end of September light now flooding the clean window. The Franklin stove squats in the middle of the room, empty and cold. Bernie carries in kindling and some split birch from the stack against the garage and builds a teepee of fire inside its mouth. The chimney still draws. No hornet's nest in the stove pipe at least. Taking a break, she goes to the kitchen to make a sandwich and fills a go-cup with coffee, then carries them back to her studio. Sitting cross-legged on the floor Bernadette opens the first box of old sepia photos and begins to sort.

"Let's have another train song then, they're good for walking. I like Leadbelly."

"Well you can't do better than 'Rock Island Line', that's for sure. Let me think, okay, 'The Midnight Special'. Are you ready?"

"Yes, you start." This time Fabian's voice booms out scratchy and deep.

Bune joins in and Fabian abandons the Leadbelly growl to play with a contralto counterpoint, weaving in and out of the angel's rock-steady backup. They're about to launch into the rollicking chorus when *whack!* Fabian hits something so impenetrable he almost knocks himself out. He rebounds, falling on his back into the turf. It sucks away his impact and forms itself around him, all gentle extrusion. To the left Bune stumbles and regains his feet.

"Oh! We made it, we're here!"

"But how do you know we're at the doorway?" asks Fabian, still supine and too simultaneously comfortable and dizzy to get up. "The doorway skips all over the place. Do you have some special demon capacity to locate it? How do you time your entry if the door is always moving?"

"You just need to stay with me. Where are you? Stand up and hold my hand again. You have to be touching me or you'll get left behind." In the dark Fabian rolls to his knees and crawls forward, wanting to feel the wall. For a moment he registers a rough surface, but then his hand flies back, slapped violently out of the way.

"Best not to meddle, it can be a little sensitive and irritable. Stand up now. Where's your hand?" Fabian slips his little hand into Bune's grip.

"Rotate, so we're facing the way we came. Good." Fabian hears the wings open and remembers their catching like a parachute on entry into his old home.

"Are we going to fall again?" he asks, his stomach clenching.

"No. Just back up slowly and don't let go of my hand, otherwise I'll have to come back for you. "They start to shuffle the few metres distance. "My wings just need to . . . Ahh! You first."

Fabian experiences an overwhelming suction and feels himself extruding backwards, leading with his tailbone. That end of him stretches as if he were taffy pulled into a long tear drop, while every part of him on the other side of the barrier snaps into a ball and seems about to implode with the pressure. With a sudden squelch he fires through and lands amoeba-like and jellified. He lies still for a long time until he feels solid enough to open his eyes. Bune leans over him, his beetle brows raised. He smiles encouragement.

"There you go. Back in shape. Entry is intense but thankfully quick. Welcome to the Gateway! The Sponsor Ring!"

Fabian squints and tries to find the ceiling but can't locate it. In the dim red light there seems no end to the space stretching above him. The floor does not cup him like the obsequious memory-foam turf. This feels resistant yet oddly rubbery. It vibrates with some distant pulse and the humid air throbs in synchrony. He rolls to his hands and knees on the uncooperative ground and smells the sulfurous stink of a hot springs. Standing, he sways like a sailor on a ship.

"It's not so supportive."

"Yes, strange after the turf isn't it?"

Fabian straightens all the way. The pulse, and then he realizes many pulses, beat and murmur around him, coming in and out of his awareness with every shift in position. A hallway stretches endlessly ahead in the red gloom. He remembers looking across the flat prairie and seeing the arch of the earth along the horizon, but this time, vertically, he can see in the distance how the corridor eventually curves out of sight. Where Corridor Nine's grey ceiling had nailed him down, here the ceiling stretches infinitely. Where Corridor Nine extended laterally into the dark, the two walls pinch him in their claustrophobic grip. Fabian guesses three Bunes could lay head to foot from wall to wall. Three demon widths.

"I don't like this place. Where can you go? At least on Corridor Nine I ran out into the dark if I wanted to, here the only escape would be up the walls, or down that hall like a hamster on a wheel."

"I like to compare the Sponsor Ring to a desert island," says Bune. "If you're afraid of the ocean, a desert island becomes a prison. If you like to swim however, it's a diving platform."

"I don't see any water."

Bune takes Fabian by the shoulders and steers him until his back touches the barrier they just fired through. Fabian flinches.

"Won't it slap me?"

"Not once you've gained entry. Now look up, look at the outside wall as far as you can see."

Fabian looks up and up.

⋖⊝⋗⋖⊝⋗⋖⊝⋗

Bernie lays out the piles of sorted photos. She wonders who held the camera for the pictures of little Fabian, her Grandmother Evelyn, "Grammy", or Grandad Herbert. Most of the snapshots are three by five inches with a white border but one large picture jumps out, an eight-by-eleven-inch print on heavier sepia paper than the others.

She picks up the image of a young woman standing in a forest of hollyhocks taller than her. The vertical sun casts everything in shadow except for the straw cloche, her shoulders, the very tip of her nose, and the t-strap shoes. Bernie thinks she can detect the sheen of a silk stocking below the longer than knee-length skirt. It looks like a loose linen jacket, neatly fitted at the shoulders, but a rose bush obscures the details. Her grandmother

142

as a young woman. The face in shadow renders her mysterious, even foreboding, pulling back instead of stepping forward and tipping her face to the sun. Bernie turns the print over and reads her grandmother's writing in faded pencil. 'Evelyn Mary on July 5, 1925 — only a few hours before my terrible accident'. Bernie looks at the image for a long time, then stands up and props it on her easel.

Sitting back down she organizes the pictures chronologically. The very youngest she can find reads, "Evelyn Mary on her way to school," in different writing this time, probably Evelyn's mother Bernadette's. The little girl poses in a chunky, cabled cardigan over her schoolgirl skirt, heavy tights bunching around her knees. She must be six or seven. A giant bow protrudes on either side of her neck, and she holds two books in the crook of her arm with her kid-gloved hand. The little girl looks about to leap with excitement, her cheeks creased by the eager confidence of her smile. Grammy on her first day of school.

Now here stands Evelyn M. under a tree, grinning with her ukulele, maybe ten years old. Evelyn on a porch swing reading a book. Holding up a heavy bicycle and smiling again under a broad-brimmed hat. How old? Maybe twelve. A serious photo of the high school graduate wearing a gown and mortarboard. The note on the back reads, "Graduated Honours, Calgary Central High." The number of photos explodes around her grandmother's late teens and her university days.

"These are amazing," mutters Bernie. She digs her phone out of her pocket and takes close-up pictures of the old photos, then attaches them to texts and sends

143

them to David. How could these be Grammy? Often, she wears a man's tie at the neck of a white-collared blouse, her signature perhaps. Laughing on a blanket at a picnic in the woods. Here she reclines on a deck chair beside another young woman, both of them stylish and excited in fur-collared coats, hairpin curls glossy on cheekbones. 'Victoria, March 1931', a girl's get-a-way. Another graduation photo, "1933, University of Alberta, BA English, Honours". Honours again, Grammy must have been pretty bright. Bernie snaps each one.

"Oh, wow." 'Dean Kimmel and Evelyn M., 1951'. It looks like a still from *The Great Gatsby*. Evelyn wears a knit swimming dress, cut high on her thighs; v-necked and sleeveless, a bathing cap covers her hair. The Errol Flynn look-alike wraps his arm around her waist and with his other hand holds the fingers of the lithesome arm she drapes over his shoulder. Her hip curves into his side, confident and supple.

Ka sha, Bernie snaps a photo and sends it to Peter. "Who knew Grammy was sexy once? And so happy? This man is not Grandad!"

✤✤✤

"Kind of like an endless card catalogue," says Fabian, looking up at the outside wall of the hallway. Row upon row of perforations, black holes into which he can fit his fist. Beside each one he can make out the imprint of a hand. From these openings come the overlapping unsynchronized beat that pulses around him. Fabian's nose wrinkles and he pulls away.

"No, come. See the writing if you look very closely? "Bune puts his hand on the boy's back and urges him

144

forward until Fabian's face is only a foot away from the throbbing wall of holes.

"What writing?"

"Don't you see? It hovers in the miasma of each gateway," and now Fabian can make out the script, handwriting like thread that lies in the faint oil-slick opalescence floating in each opening. He reaches up to his forehead for a moment and then laughs. He says to Bune, "Glasses, I forgot. No longer required. What do they all say? So many. Where would you start?"

"They tell each sponsor's story, at least the most pertinent conditions for, how shall I say, a prospective applicant. Look here, I brought us into the section of your kin, there are many who will be familiar to you. For example, your grandmother Bernadette."

"Oh!" Eagerly Fabian steps over towards Bune but is perplexed to see just one diagonal line of writing across the aperture. He reads, grins at Fabian, "I recognize her writing!" *Temporary leave of absence. Possible future sponsorships accepted. Please check back and best wishes on your next assignment.* "Oh, that's too bad. You mean possibly she could have been my new mother?"

"Yes. If you put your hand in the palm print, you can remember her a moment." Fabian fits his small hand into the indent. His lids quiver shut and a beatific smile creeps over his face.

"Those apples off the tree behind the kitchen, creamed salmon on toast. She always smelled like toast. Amazing! I can feel her; loyal, reliable, no matter if you made a mistake. *Oh, her laugh.* My Gran always had my back. I trusted her." He takes his hand down and steps

145

back, his small body slumps. "Now please, now could I have my tears back?"

"Look here though, try this one. So many options." Bune steers him gently back to the wall. "I know you wouldn't want to attempt this one again so soon, Evelyn Mary Eddy, but just out of curiosity. Anyhow, it reads: 'Extended leave of absence.'"

Fabian shudders, raises his hand slowly to the imprint. As soon as his hand is in place, he starts wincing like a lab rat undergoing electric shock stimuli.

"So sharp! So angry, I never understood why she was *so angry*, frustrated! The goddamn monkey suits she used to put me in. Little Fabian, my hair greased down, precious, perfect boy. But when we got home . . . No, not the boot of the car again!" His eyes fly open and he pulls his hand away. "God, I hated grocery shopping with her. If I messed up, into the boot of the car for the ride home." Bune clucks in horror. "That's nothing, she used to pull her orphanage manoeuvre when I was really bad," Fabian chuckles. "Like the time I set fire to a paper bag of dog shit on Mr. Ridley's front porch. You can imagine what Mr. Ridley did when I rang the bell and ran away . . . " He grins up at the angel. "Of course, she never saw the humour. She'd hand me this little suitcase and tell me to go pick out two of my favourite toys, pack a toothbrush, and some underwear. Then I had to sit on the front step while she phoned the orphanage lady to come pick me up."

"Good Lord, seriously?"

"Yes! By the fourth time when no one came, I figured out she was phoning her friend Eunice. She thought it was a funny game. What I don't understand Bune, is why I ever chose her?"

"Sometimes a sponsor has contradictory aspects to their personality. Evelyn was vivacious and intelligent, even humorous once. Perhaps that's what attracted you. Put your hand back on a moment. Let's just see." Reluctantly Fabian complies. His face softens begrudgingly.

"She really was bloody smart, and you're right, definitely *naughty* in college, sexy and adventurous. But oh, yes, the little detail of the car accident after her final year, I must have chosen to ignore that, she was just so magnetic."

"The Model T, that flew over a washed-out bridge."

"Yes, that changed everything, for her, and as a result for me too, I guess. A sad story all around."

"But now you understand suffering, do you not? Let's try another one."

"Could Margaret possibly be here?" Fabian asks.

Bune touches the wall and pulls down with a flicking motion of his fingers.

"I love this scroll feature." The column of orifices flashes downward past Fabian's dazzled eyes. Bune reaches out again and stops the motion. "Here, Margaret Neff MacComber. No, sadly also unavailable, but if you want to go down memory lane?"

"No," Fabian turns away.

"Just a moment, ah. Margaret's and your daughter, Bernadette MacComber." Fabian rotates back, stares sadly.

"Little Bernie." The diagonal thread of script reads: 'Sorry, just too fucking tired to accept sponsorships at this time, also sperm donor deactivated. Please try back,

147

but at a much later date.' Fabian lays his hand over the imprint and closes his eyes for a long while. Finally, he looks up at Bune.

"She's a combination of Margaret and my grandma; the creative bohemian jive of her mother, with the steady flavour of my Gran, but fiercer. She's like a bear; she'd eat anyone if they hurt her kids." He sighs and lets his hand drop. "So much like home though, or as close to home as I'll ever get."

"Well anyhow, you understand the idea. Obviously, there are endless options. When we come back, we can do an exhaustive search until you're satisfied with your choice. Time won't be an issue. But I think we'd better return to Corridor Nine now, we still need to work on lesson three. I'm afraid you might find it challenging. But now you know what we're working towards, yes?" Fabian nods. "Excellent, good for motivation."

Fabian looks up at the columns and columns of conceivable lifetimes, around the curve of the Sponsor Ring. He listens to the soft throb of possibilities. Finally, he lets Bune take his hand. They turn to the bald face of the interior wall.

"Ready?"

"I guess so."

"Then rotate." Fabian hears the big wings rustle and snap open again.

"Back up slowly, and you first.

It's seven o'clock on Sunday morning and Bernie smiles up at the bedroom ceiling listening to the silence of the house and Peter breathing beside her. She slips out of bed and gets into her flannel pajamas, then pads past Angus. He cocks an unbelieving eyebrow at her, gets up, rotates, and lies down with nose under his tail.

In the kitchen she turns on the under-cabinet lights and fills the kettle. Today the guys from A.D.D. will meet her at the old house to gut and empty the basement. She imagines her father's manifesto will fill another dumpster, but then she will be finished with that whole business and a realtor can list the house

Bernie gets the slow cooker out of the pantry and sets it to high. From the fridge she retrieves the ten-pound beef brisket she bought yesterday at the butchers. No more pizza for her children. No more bagged instant dinners, macaroni and cheese out a box, KFC. No. No bloody more. She has completed the whole arduous business of Fabian, and today she will come back home, come back to her life. Bernie dowses the massive slab of meat in paprika, cumin, chipotle chili, brown sugar and salt. She wedges it into the slow cooker and puts on the lid. By six o'clock it will be fork tender and falling apart. Leaning against the counter, she eats a bowl of granola and then has a shower.

"See you later." Bernie kisses Peter on the shoulder, leaning over him, sleeping on his side.

"You going?"

"Yes, this won't take long. I should be back by ten. Are you sure you have to go to work on a Sunday?"

"Mmm, have to finish the specs. I don't have to be there until nine thirty though. Eben can keep an eye on the kids for a bit."

Angus sits up as she leaves the bedroom. "You stay," she says, "we'll go for a walk with the kids in the afternoon."

"Why isn't she moving much, Lola? I want to take her out. You said I could hold her tomorrow, and now its tomorrow and I want to hold her! Come on, you promised."

"I don't know Moira, I think we should let her sleep. She's tired lately. Maybe her diet is too low in protein now. She hasn't gotten any mealworms in a month, but I don't want to ask Mom because, well, you know."

"Mom is going through a tough time," recites Mo. "We need to give her a break. I'm hungry; Daddy's oatmeal was disgusting. I never eat oatmeal. *Mom* knows that." The frizzy-haired seven-year-old pulls her knees under her chin and hugs them to her chest, looking around Lola's tidy bedroom. On this overcast morning the only warmth comes from the anemic-yellow glow of the heat lamp.

"Well come on, let's go make hot chocolate or something," Lola leads the way into the kitchen, where Louis digs through cupboards in search of anything edible.

"I'm starving, Daddy's oatmeal was really bad today. So slimy! Where does Eben hide the Ichiban?"

"Upstairs under his bed, but he said we've almost finished it. Go ask him." In a few moments he returns triumphant with one last cup of instant noodles.

"Shotgun on the last Ichiban!"

Mo's eyebrows hunker down, her lips pout.

"That's not fair, just because you thought of it first. I want one too . . . "

"I called shotgun," says Louis.

Later they sit perched on stools and the rolling chair, pulled up to the computer watching *Harry Potter and the*

Deathly Hallows. Moira covers up her head with the couch throw.

"Why do we have to watch this, I hate it. I want to watch air bending; let's switch to *Avatar*."

"You're just being a chicken," says Louis. "Plug your ears until we get through the wedding part."

"I hate the wedding. There's that snake and the death eaters. Last time I couldn't sleep. It's not fair. Why do you guys always get to pick?" Keeping her eyes squeezed shut and her fingers in her ears, Mo wiggles out of the chair and pull away from the tangling blanket. "La la la la la la la la," she drowns out the soundtrack as she walks down the hall. Her bedroom looks so dark and messy that although she contemplates working on her Lego animal rescue centre, she keeps walking. She stops outside Lola's door and opens it and looks inside this feminine enclave. First, she tiptoes to the desk and one by one opens the bottles of essential oils. Don't spill she tells herself, sniffing. Lavender, mandarin, summer blossom, pumpkin pie. She likes pumpkin pie best but restrains from rubbing it on her pulse points, Lola would smell it and then the shit would hit the fan, as daddy liked to say. She manages to screw all the lids back on successfully. Encouraged Moira looks around the room. Cynthia lies sleeping in her cage. Cynthia wouldn't mind being held just because she's sleeping. Why would she?

Her eyes settle on the thick books on Lola's bottom shelf. Those will do. Mo takes five of them and stacks them up beside the cage. Stepping up she can reach in now and touch the bedding. Just because you're seven doesn't mean you don't know how to handle a hedgehog. Expertly she slides her small hands under Cynthia's soft

151

belly and lifts, expecting the hedgehog to twitch or raise her head, but she must be really tired. I'll just hold her a little while, she thinks turning around on the pile of books. I'll go make a nest of Lola's throw pillows and turn on her mermaid lamp, and then . . . Mo stops, or tries to stop midstep off the books, because Angus stands in the doorway staring. Why hadn't she remembered to shut the door? Lola always said to shut the door.

��

"I have to eat oatmeal again? That's the fourth time!"
"Well, the turf in its wisdom is trying to assist you with your last lesson."

"Stoicism, persistence, sticking it out, "recites Fabian.

"The boredom wears on you I know, but staying with that, bearing it, realizing it will end, that's the whole point."

"Oh, I hate this. What do we have to do today, sort more clouds by category? Actually anything, please, but not another walking and breathing meditation; really I can't handle that."

"You realize, don't you, what's at stake?"

"Uh, something about not giving up this time?"

"That's right. If you fail an assignment, take your life by your own hand instead of sticking it out, then off to the mulch pit with you. No more chances. Stoicism and patience are required to complete an assignment successfully; that is why you need to work through these exercises. Do you want to pick another form for me to take?" Bune wheedles and the two extra heads pop out of his shoulders. "Eeny meeny miney mo?"

"Oh whatever, maybe the griffon will stimulate a little adrenalin. Do that one."

⟶⟨⟩⟶

When Bernie pulls into the driveway of her parent's home, she sees Derek and Troy reclining in the Adirondack chairs on the back deck. Their down vests look good and dirty. They smoke cigarettes, and when she comes up the stairs Derek smiles with all his pointy, greying teeth. They butt out their cigarettes in the barrel planter.

"Morning," they say. Troy yawns in the depths of his hoody and rubs his eyes with a fist.

"We always seem to meet on grey days," says Bernie.

"Yeah. How've you been?" Derek's bushy eyebrows hunker down over the bridge of his nose as he stares into her face.

"Better, I'm feeling a lot better, thanks to you guys getting that mess cleared out for one thing. How have you been?"

"Good, good. Business has been steady. Hey, Troy?"

"Yeah, we've been working pretty steady, but getting breaks too."

"Today won't be as bad as last time. It's kind of bizarre what you'll find in the basement, though. Let me show you." Bernie unlocks the back door with the blue key on her key chain. They walk through the empty kitchen, and in the basement stairwell she pulls the beaded chord. The old light bulb ignites one more time. They descend the stairs, and she switches on the other light.

"Holy shit," says Troy.

"Yeah. My dad wrote a book and printed a lot of copies. Unfortunately, his writing was crazy rambling by the end of his life. Could we fill your truck and take it somewhere for recycling? I feel bad throwing out so much paper."

"Sure, there's a recycling station at the dump."

Bernie leads the way over the books and through the jagged hole in the drywall.

"Wow," they say in unison.

"My dad's old acid prints. So, you see, these two partitions need to come down. I'll take down all the posters. Could the rocking boat and that little stove go to the Sally Ann?"

"Your dad was a bizarrely cool dude." Troy stares at the turquoise iris print. "You gonna throw these out?"

"You can take some of them home if you want." She starts to pull out the pushpins and take the remaining posters down. Bernie stops when she gets to her father's sketch of Francis the House Mouse. They guys are starting to fill their arms with books. "Derek?"

"Yeah?"

"Do you have a knife?"

"Sure." He sticks his head through the hole.

"Could you cut around this drawing? I think I'd like to keep it."

"No worries."

When Bernie heads up the stairs, she looks back at them.

"Have you had breakfast?"

"Uh, no. I mean, we're fine," says Derek.

"I'll just run by McDonald's."

When Bernie returns Derek comes into the kitchen from the living room.

"What do you want to do with those blue bins full of pictures?"

"Could you put them on the porch?" She follows him into the living room. Derek picks up the first one, but the half-open flap on the top catches on his vest and flops open. Prints slither onto the floor.

"Oh sorry!" He kneels and starts gathering them up. She sees him glance at the images. He studies Bernie and David laughing and balancing on the log in Kootenay Lake. "Wow. That looks like fun." His eyes track from the photo up to Bernie, matching the faces. "I went to camp once."

No, she thinks. That was my summer every year.

"I got egg McMuffins and coffee. There's cream and sugar in the bottom of the bag." Bernie turns and goes to the kitchen. She stares out the window and sees Eva Gotslieg's light on.

Eva comes to the door in a magenta tracksuit.

"Oh, what good timing! Come in, I just took some muffins out. How is the house going, dear? How are you?"

Bernie sits down at the kitchen table and studies Eva's rooster and chicken salt and pepper shakers. Her stomach is in a knot again. She shakes her head at the muffin, but accepts coffee.

"I keep thinking I'm done with this, that I have some resolution, but then another memory comes up, and guilt floods me. I don't know how to get free of the guilt!"

"Whatever do you mean dear?"

"I was just looking at all the photos my father took of us. Our childhood looks so idyllic, so lucky, all the nature, the art, our cabin . . ."

"He did some things right of course, or your mother did. But later you couldn't have had him around your

155

children. He'd become too unstable. Your first duty is always to your children. You can't feel guilty about that."

Bernie hovers her nose over the coffee and breathes in the steam.

"I think I would feel a lot better if I could find his gun collection. I've searched everywhere and I can't find it. He had close to twenty guns, a hand gun, a machine gun, a crossbow, and a lot of rifles." Even so, leaving Eva's house and wandering back through the old yard, she feels better. The guys have brought plastic crates from their truck and now carry them filled with books. I am done, she thinks, pretty close to done. She asks the guys to lock up and leave the key with Eva when they finish. Bernie gets in her van and drives home to spend Sunday with her kids.

Eben takes the duvet off his head and pulls the earbuds out. He should be downstairs, but he can hear *Harry Potter* still playing. They're fine. Just as long as he gets downstairs before his mother comes back. His phone vibrates on the bed and the screen lights up. He doesn't want to look. Madison.

"Please text me? Sorry I told Leanne and now she knows you know, but I just really need your help talking to Jake, and if you tell him he'll understand. Please? Sorry, sorry, sorry"

"Fuck," says Eben. He rolls over and sticks his head under his pillow. In a little while he pulls the phone under with him and opens the calculator function. He blew the chemistry test. One more time he punches in his marks and the total comes back again, sixty-one percent.

"Fuck," says Eben. His eighty-percent average is history now, how will he ever make that up? He feels sick and shaky, he should eat something, he should eat something with protein. He should get out of bed. His phone flashes.

"please?????"

"K"

"what does that mean?"

"'K, I'll talk to him."

"when?"

"Monday

LOVE YOU!"

"'K"

He sits up and swings his legs off the bed, holds his haggard face in his hands. He reaches for his phone.

"But then he'll think I agree with you, and really, I don't think I do."

Five minutes later.

"Leanne will think you're a prick. All the girls will think you're a prick."

Eben looks out the window at the heavy clouds, the unmoving branches. He watches a squirrel run across the high wire, do a little trapeze act. He picks up his phone again.

"'K"

"love you"

"Fuck off," says Eben to the glowing screen, and goes to take a shower.

Moira half falls off the books and Angus wags his tail. His hackles rise and he stares at the hedgehog like there is no one else in the room.

"No, no! No Angus!" Her voice comes out a prayerful squeak. They circle, she holds Cynthia up above her head. Angus wags his tail and growls happily, deep in his throat. He pounces at Moira's bare feet and scratches them with his blunt black nails.

"Ow! *No Angus,*" she pleads, her eyes smarting. He wags and growls and doesn't take his eyes off Cynthia. At least now she is between the dog and the door. Very slowly she takes one hand down, and while still holding Cynthia aloft reaches with her other to the top of the bookcase. Her fingers close on something stuffed and furry. She throws it.

"Fetch Angus!" The dog turns for a second and Moira whips out the door and pulls it shut behind her, her heart pounding and Angus snuffling and scratching through the wood. She looks towards the living room. They've paused the movie.

"I have to go to the bathroom. Just wait," says Louis.

The bathroom is between the living room and Moira, but the back door is only a step away. Like lightening she grabs Louis' rubber boots and a coat from the floor and darts outside. She shuffles to the right until she's out of sight and stares panting at the yard. The concrete burns her feet with cold, so she slips into Louis' boots. What coat did she pick up? Her dad's down vest. She puts it on and it hangs below her knees, the armholes gaping to her waist, but Mo hunkers low and skitters past the livingroom windows until she comes to the cotoneaster hedge. Home sailing now, she takes the trail behind all the bushes along the neighbour's fence until she gets to the tree house. With one hand she climbs the wooden ladder, pops open the hatch, and rolls onto the floor of the cedar-scented room. She kicks the trapdoor shut and carefully lays Cynthia on her chest. Cynthia seems different. So rubbery. Moira has never seen her like this, flat on her belly with all four vestigial limbs splayed like a hide tacked to a wall. As soon as they're watching the movie again, she'll sneak back and put her in her cage. But what will she do about Angus?

"Okay, let's try a more physical tack. All right? Just physical endurance, and the baby will provide some distraction, then we'll get back to the mental endurance, but you can't bail again, okay? You have to do this."

"What do you want me to do then?" Fabian flops onto his back. "I can see practising to improve one's knowledge, or courage, or strength, but why the fuck do I have to practise boredom?"

"Because life is boring, long stretches of it. People learn at different rates so there's always a supplementary margin added in. At times nothing but endurance will get you through. So, what I want you to do this time is take Bernie and walk her all the way around Corridor Nine. Do a lap with her."

Fabian looks doubtfully over at the screen behind which baby Bernie stands frozen at the tender age of two.

"You've got to be kidding?"

Bernie opens the door and hears the screaming. For a moment she can't sort out the tangle of voices coming from Lola's room. She runs down the hall. Eben and Lola and Louis stand in front of Cynthia's cage, Angus sits watching the show and looks quizzically over his shoulder at Bernie when she rushes in. Lola is gripping her head and rocking on her feet while Eben rubs her back.

"Oh no, oh no, oh no! He's eaten her, he's eaten Cynthia!"

"Mommy!" Lola rushes Bernie, lands sobbing on her chest.

"Eben what's going on? I thought you were watching the kids?"

Eben looks at the ground and scuffs his feet.

"It seems that, uhm, somehow, while I was taking a shower, the dog got in and now we can't find the hedgehog."

"Okay, everyone calm down." She pushes Lola away from her chest, holds her firmly by the shoulders. "Lola, I don't think we should jump to conclusions. Are you sure? I mean Cynthia would be a hard pill to swallow and . . . " she looks at Angus. "Angus looks fine, there's no blood anywhere. You think he got in the cage? The stand is pretty tall. Who stacked up those books?" The kids all look at her. Angus wags.

"Moira. Where's Moira?" They stare. "You guys stay here, I'll go find her. I think something's up." Bernie walks fast from room to room, calling and looking in closets and under beds. She checks the furnace room, the rumpus room, even looks inside the washing machine. Her heart starts to pound, and she runs outside. "Moira?" she shouts at the top of her lungs. The greenhouse? Her studio? But first she tries the tree house, scrambles up the ladder, pops the hatch. White-faced Mo sits in a corner, her hands folded over the hedgehog on her chest.

"Mo! God you scared me. What's going on, honey? What are you doing, why have you . . . ?" From the back door Lola calls. Bernie turns to the window and answers.

"She's here, Cynthia's safe." In a moment Lola flies up the ladder, scrambles across the floor and wrestles the hedgehog from Mo.

"Oh, Mommy something's wrong. She's not moving at all, she's all rubbery. Is she dead? Oh no! I know what's happened. Moira's cooled her off out here and forced her into an unnatural state of hibernation. I can't believe this has happened!" She stares at her little sister. Mo twitches in horror.

"I didn't mean to," whispers Mo, and the tears start rolling down her face.

"Let's just stay calm Lola. Are you sure? I thought hedgehogs hibernated."

"Not African hedgehogs!"

"Okay we'll get Cynthia back under her heat lamp and go Google what to do when you've cooled down an African hedgehog. Come on Mo, it's going to be okay, come inside."

In the nook she realizes she can't get onto the computer.

"Did Daddy change the password? What's the password?"

"Mortise," they say in unison.

"Mortise?"

"Yeah, like a 'mortise and tenon'. It's a kind of joint," says Eben.

Bernie Googles "hibernation African hedgehog."

"Oh dear. They shouldn't be cooled off. It's called aestivation. They slow down but not enough to conserve their energy sufficiently . . . uuhh, shit, can be fatal. I mean serious. How long has she been acting like this, just today?"

"Well, she's been funny all week, sleepy and not eating much, but not unconscious!"

"Is her heat lamp broken?" They all hurry to Lola's room, Bernie looks at the yellow bulb in the aluminum shade. "Who put this in, heat lamps are red. This is one of those yellow bulbs that Daddy uses on the porch. You know, the no bug kind."

Eben stands behind them.

"I did. The old one broke, and I, I thought the colour didn't matter . . . "

"So, you mean, maybe it wasn't me? It wasn't my fault?" asks Mo.

"It's no one's fault," says Bernie. "If anything, it's because I've not been paying attention to you guys. I blame myself. Let's not worry about whose fault it is, let's just get Cynthia to the vet." Quickly Bernie unbuttons the top of her denim shirt. She takes Cynthia from Lola and pulls forward the elastic fabric of her yoga top. Carefully she inserts the hedgehog belly facing her chest. The prickles protrude between her breasts and through the lycra. "Body heat is best," she says, the children agog. "Now everyone into the van." Where did Eben go? Bernie grabs her car keys off the shelf and herds the other three out the door.

"It would help if I had candy or something to entice her. A puppy, or better yet a stroller!" Fabian stares after the toddling form of blonde fuzz-head Bernie, piping a nonsensical tune as she staggers off into the dark again.

"*You* must be the distraction; go charm her." Fabian groans and looks at the griffon sitting on the turf beside him. The eagle head yawns, stretching open its black beak. "I might just take a short nap. You two carry on and I'll catch up . . . "

Again, Fabian follows her.

"Bernie, Bernie. Come here baby." She looks over her shoulder and smiles her drooling grin. With a gleeful squawk she breaks into a gallop. Fabian wishes he'd been given something older than a four-year-old body. He suspects Bernie's "capacity to exhaustion" has not been restored to *her,* while his most certainly has. He sprints to catch up, then takes a flying leap and pins her to the turf. Baby squeals in surprise, then roars in affronted rage. She flails her heels and won't get up no matter how Fabian pulls on her hands or plays peekaboo making asinine smiley faces. Bloody hell. Finally, he just picks her up and starts staggering back towards the Membrane. She writhes like a salmon and flips out of his arms, falls to the turf with a thump. Then she really starts to bellow.

"Bune!" shouts Fabian. "Bune? Where the hell *are you?*"

"I feel itchy again," Louis says to Lola in the back seat.

"Mom! I think Louis is having an allergic reaction." Bernie looks in the rear-view mirror.

"What's that, Lola?" She concentrates on changing lanes. The hedgehog intruding on her cleavage requires a more ginger handling of the steering wheel. She finally moves into the right lane and looks into the rear-view mirror again. Studies their faces. "Did you say, 'allergic reaction'?"

"Yes. Louis is getting itchy again. He's been itching all week. He gets this rash."

"Good Lord, how bad? Why hasn't anyone told me?" She studies his freckled face in the mirror. Eerie familiarity floods her. "Louis, how do you feel, are you all right?" She can see the hives on his neck, how they creep onto his cheeks. His face breaks into a sweat and his eyes grow big with panic.

"I feel really sick Mom!"

"Oh, boy!" The van fires down Sixteenth Avenue. They cross the bridge over the Bow River and there is nowhere to pull over for half a mile. She looks at Louis' face again and makes her decision. Trying for a somewhat gradual angle, she cranks the wheel right and takes the curb. The van lurches up and onto the shoulder. Bernie hauls on the parking brake and gets her seat belt off. "Take his seat belt off quick Lola!" She opens her door and runs around to the other side of the van, throws the sliding door open and drags Louis out. She's got him in front of her facing away. "Remember? Like old times buddy."

"I can't poop right on the road!"

"Can you wait?"

"No Momma!" Bernie pulls his pants down to his ankles and grabs him firmly behind the knees. She squats until her elbows lock on her thighs and she's got him in the floating toilet pose. And just in the nick of time.

"Do what you've got to do buddy. No one can see, the van's blocking the view." Very soon he finishes expelling. "Lola, can you find the wipes? That was a close one." Lola pulls wipes from the plastic container and waves them out the door like the queen. "Put them right in my hand, I can't move here. Okay, all cleaned up. Back in the van buddy." Bernie washes her hands with another wipe, looks around and finds a big rock to cover up the evidence. Then she opens the hatch and digs the first-aid kit out of the compartment under the floor. Calamine with antihistamine. In the back seat she anoints his welts and checks his chest and back.

"This is the same reaction you had after Chinese food when you were four. Do you remember, Louis? When we figured out MSG didn't agree with you. But what could have set you off this time, I don't let that stuff in the house anymore." Bernie looks down, pulls back the edge of her yoga top, and studies Cynthia. "Okay, let's get moving." In the front seat she buckles up, slides the shoulder strap behind her back, to not further traumatize the hedgehog, and when a big enough break in the traffic opens, she humps the van back onto the highway.

"Oh, I didn't even phone them! I guess we should let them know we're coming. Lola, please get my phone out of my purse and dial Dr. Randall."

"I look in contacts, right?"

"Yes, but it's under 'veterinarian' not 'Randall'." She looks back at them lined up on the bench seat. "You kids didn't break into that box of Ichiban for the Food Bank . . . ?"

☙❧☙

"How could you possibly expect me to do a full rotation with a tyrannical, noncompliant midget. Where do you get these ideas? Is it in your training manual for demons? 'Torture unfortunate captive of Corridor Nine with impossible feats of babysitting.'" Fabian snorts and stomps along beside the griffon. Bernie sleeps curled on the fur between the creature's wings.

Bune clacks his beak open and shut, looks sideways out of his beady eye.

"At least you got a break from the boredom. You *are* a hard one to please."

⋦⊕⋧

In the veterinarian's examination room Bernie watches her three children and feels the unmoving cool of Cynthia against her chest. Lola hugs herself and paces, Mo sits pale and concave in her chair, and Louis, waits calm, welty, and spackled with the bubble-gum coloured calamine.

"Guys?" They look up. "I just want you to know, you don't have to feel guilty about this. I've been so preoccupied with the old house and the issues with my dad that I, I forgot about you for awhile. I've not been on the job and I'm really, really sorry." They watch her. "So, whatever happens, you need to know that I'm back now and you don't have to worry. I won't go away again. Whatever happens I will handle it, and you'll all be okay."

From three directions they run at Bernie and contact like magnets to steel, their arms tangle around her, they fight for skin space. She encircles the three heads, kiss their hair. Louis and Mo smell like horses. When did they

166

last have a bath? Tap tap, a knock at the door. Dr. Randall peeks her head in, smiling.

⟿⟾⟿

After another bowl of oatmeal and returning baby Bernie to her original egg-wrapped form, Bune switches back to full angel format.

"We are running short on time. Before we sleep, we'll try one more walking and breathing meditation."

"Oh no." Fabian groans and rolls his eyes.

"Think of the long-term goal, Tadpole, *think* how much you've already accomplished. Stand up. If you pull this off, we just have one more day of exercises."

"What kind of exercises?"

"Being in the moment, dropping into the sensations of your body, feeling your breath as it enters and leaves your nostrils . . . "

"Jesus Christ! Another day of that?"

"Yes! I can think of a lot of worse things to do with your time. Mindfulness greatly increases quality of life. Now follow after me. With each breath feel the turf on the soles of your feet. Inhale and notice where the sensation of the breath most easily registers in your consciousness. Your nostrils, your throat, your rib cage?"

"La, la, la" intones Fabian under his breath as he follows. "La, la, lalala . . . " A quarter of the way around one rotation of the lifetimes of man, Bune pauses in the rapture of his breathing and, stepping back, looks at Fabian. He walks far behind him dragging his feet, stopping now and then to do some ballistic bouncing, or to scratch. Bune rubs the heels of his hands into his eye sockets and stretches out his cramped wings. He materializes a cigarette and carries on. This time with a walking and smoking meditation.

⊷⊶⊷

Bernie looks out the windows as she minces white onion for the salsa. The grey clouds hang even heavier in the last hour before dark. No birds sing, no wind stirs, everything waits. She takes a deep breath and looks around the snug kitchen and the living room, glowing in the light of the lamp. A fire crackles in the grate. All the kids are supervising the hedgehog. Dr. Randall rehydrated Cynthia with a saline and glucose drip and sent them home with the hedgehog strapped to a gel-filled heating disk, good for twelve hours of gradual warming.

"Her heart rate has slowed, but its good and strong. I think she'll pull out of aestivation. Just give her time to warm up." An hour ago, a shout rang out of the bedroom, and they all ran into the kitchen gibbering.

"She's opened her eyes Mommy!"

"She yawned!"

What a miracle. Euphoric with relief Bernie puts together her taco dinner. She heaps the shredded steaming brisket into a casserole, then takes the corn tortillas out of the oven and stacks them on a plate. The table is set, and covered with bowls of condiments; chopped avocado, grated cheese, shredded lettuce, black olives. Bernie squeezes lime juice over the tomatoes, adds the red pepper, salt, and chopped cilantro, gives it a stir and carries the bowl to the table. She shouts for them to come and in a minute they all stand staring.

"Wow, tacos!" says Peter. "Let's dig in!"

⊷⊶⊷

168

I wish I could sing, thinks Fabian. That was really fun, the whole scene used to be a lot more fun. And what's up with the food? Would he get nothing but oatmeal now for the duration of his stay? He squints ahead and sees Bune disappearing in the distance. He hurries up a bit but still wants to stay out of earshot, so he can hum. He thinks of train songs and remembers how Margaret used to sing Elizabeth Cotton's "Freight Train" to the children at night. How did that go again? *Freight train, freight train, run so fast . . .*

Fabian stops dead. Unbelievably something new, an actual object in this objectless world lies in front of his feet. A white feather. Not one of Bune's big wing feathers. One of the smaller more interior ones. It lies curled and so delicate it barely maintains contact with the turf. Entertaining that baby would have been a lot easier with a feather. Fabian bends down and picks it up. He brushes it against his cheek, his eyelids, and tries to distinguish what makes it different from the feathers of home. More like a leaf he decides, but so silky and light. It fits exactly into his palm. If he closes his fingers no one would even know it was there. He wonders if Bune would want it back and possessiveness overwhelms him. Maybe owning a feather is illegal on Corridor Nine. Too distracting. Suddenly feeling very happy he walks faster, humming. Looking far ahead he sees Bune has reached the two eggs, and that's when the idea hits him. His heart pounds. He almost breaks into a run but controls himself. Very sedately he walks heel to toe, breathing in, feeling the breath expanding his rib cage, another step as he exhales serenely through his nostrils. All the while he's frantically thinking. When he finally returns to camp, he

169

exhales peacefully one more time just to show the angel. Bune watches him, jaw dropped.

"I think I got the hang of it," says Fabian. "Can I go to sleep now?"

"You're not hungry? You don't want another bowl of oatmeal?"

"No!"

"Well good night then." The angel lies down several paces away with his back to him. Fabian studies his wings. He wonders where the feather fell out. He feels the soft treasure in his hand as he watches the Membrane go through its sunset progression one last time. Soon the first white twinkle of a star pops up in the teal and olive-green sky, and finally Bune's back rises and falls, predictable as waves.

Silently he rolls to his hands and knees and then very carefully stands up. Bune's breathing continues unceasing. Fabian takes courage and slowly takes a big step backwards then another, and another. Finally, he turns. Orient yourself due black, he thinks, squaring himself as best he can in the last vestiges of light from the Membrane. Miraculously the turf transforms into corduroy beneath his feet. Follow the grain and you can't get lost. Fabian turns and runs.

I am Fabian MacComber he thinks over and over as the blackness bears down on him. I am Fabian MacComber escape artist extraordinaire. To mark the time, he goes through all the songs he and Bune sang in exactly the same order, but this time silently in his head. He has the little feather in his hand and though his heart pounds, it is with excitement more than fear. Finally, he gets to Midnight Special and slowly paces forward; he should be

170

there any moment now . . . His outstretched hand touches something hard and rough. Whack! It gets slapped away. Fabian chuckles.

He inhales a few deep breaths. Now. He must do it now. He must be brave. His arm shakes as he raises the feather towards the wall. He leans forward until the feather makes contact. Nothing happens. Fabian holds his breath, leans forward even more. His arm nearly rips from his socket. The wall swallows him.

❧❧❧

The three younger kids lean against Bernie on Lola's bed. Moira on her left, Louis on her right, and Lola lying sideways with her head on her mother's leg for a pillow. She closes *The Wind in the Willows*.

"Why is Toad such an idiot?" asks Louis.

"Short attention span, high need for stimulation, and too much ego, I guess. You guys did really well with that, I thought the language might be too hard."

"Nah, I understood the feeling. Can you sing me 'Freight Train' now ,Mom? Like you used to when I was little?"

"You still remember that, Mo?"

"Yes! 'Freight Train' was my song and Louis got 'I've Been Workin' On the Railroad'."

"What did I sing for Lola and Eben? Oh, 'Good Night Irene', that's an old Leadbelly tune. But I'll start with 'Freight Train'. Do you remember the words?"

"Sing it all sad and quavery like Elizabeth Cotton," says Moira.

Bernie begins, and her voice cracks as it eases into the melancholy longing of Elizabeth Cotton's song of escape.

Fabian stands before the wall of sponsors. He keeps taking deep breaths to hold back the sensation of drowning in the sulpher stinking air. The holes go on endlessly in every direction. How can he choose? He keeps looking over his shoulder, expecting Bune to shoot through the wall at any moment. Quickly he puts his hand in a palm print, reads the name floating on the surface of the orifice. Jeannie Stapleton. The rounded clumsy handwriting disgusts him. What incredibly bland cooking. He tries another. A frantic schedule. No unstructured time, and a nanny to boot. Fish sticks and Froot Loops. No!

Fabian keeps trying. He wishes Bune were here to help him make his choice, but there's no going back now. I just want to go home he thinks, and immediately, the column of orifices starts flashing downwards before his eyes. He blinks and reads the diagonal handwriting, "Sorry, just too fucking tired to accept sponsorships at this time . . . "It's Bernie. Fabian stares hopelessly at the letters quivering there, then he steps forward. The writing looks so like thread. He stares at the 'e' at the end of *much later date*. Is it possible? He reaches forward and pinches the tail of the e with his thumb and forefinger. Yes, it rolls between his fingers. Very gently he starts to pull, and the letters come away like embroidery pulled from a cloth, pop, pop, pop, stitch by stitch, word by word. With the diagonal writing gone, the gateway pulses quietly. Open.

Fabian looks over his shoulder. No Bune. He looks back. "If you like to swim however, it's a diving platform . . . " He puts his hands together in prayer position, inserts them halfway.

172

"I took care of you last time," he says to the hole in the wall named Bernadette MacComber. "Now it's my turn." Fabian closes his eyes and bends his knees. "I'm going in," he says, and jumps.

᧐᧐᧐

"What a fantastic day!" Bernie lies on her back, chortling in the dark.

"Really? The hedgehog nearly died, Lola and Mo were close to homicide, Louis shit himself on the side of the highway, and you did the final cleanout of your dad's house . . . "

"Exactly!"

"It sounds arduous to me."

"Nah, that's nothing! I can handle anything they throw at me. Finally, I'm really done with my dad. I'm back on the job, 'I'm back in the saddle again'!" She laughs, pauses for a moment. "No pun intended."

Silence.

"No pun taken. Although I have to say, it's been a while, I mean, almost five weeks . . . "

"Hmm." Bernie rolls towards him, squidges across the pillow and sticks her nose in his hair. "I really appreciate," she mumbles "how you're always so clean." She works her way around to the skin behind his ear, starts biting him gently down the side of his neck with her lips pulled over her teeth, like an old guy with his dentures out. She pauses. "You're right actually, what an arduous day. I think I'm sleepy."

"In that case you need to be careful."

Bernie rubs her cheek into the hair of his chest, breathes in how he smells.

"How am I to interpret these mixed messages?" asks Peter.

"I'll leave that to you."

Later they listen to the rain pelting down, branches flailing against the walls.

"The funny thing is, we didn't find them," Bernie murmurs.

"Find what?"

"We couldn't find my dad's gun collection."

"Maybe he sold them, to pay for his habit, you know?"

"I guess so," says Bernie, and in a little while they both burrow into sleep.

The morning dawns rinsed sunny and clear. Brushing her hair at the bathroom window Bernadette pulls up the blind and surveys the destruction of the night. What a storm. Branches strewn everywhere. Pine cones litter the hood of her car, and puddles of rain steam, warmer than the October air.

She tries to remember her dream, so distinct it woke her in the early hours of the morning. An immense bell tolling in a steeple, and then that funny scene, standing on a railway platform with that very resolute man. She'd said to him, "I wasn't thinking of going on a trip," and he'd replied, "Don't worry, I've packed everything you'll need in this duffle bag." She'd unzipped the bag and it was stuffed with immaculate cream-coloured doll clothes, she could barely close it with the big brass zipper. Bernie looks at her watch. So late! She pulls on her jeans and runs to wake up the kids.

Bernie walks across the wet grass to her studio, picking up the branches the wind flailed off the birch. She snaps them into shorter lengths and piles them with the firewood against the garage. When they dry out, they'll make good kindling. Heading for her studio she stops. What is that? Something silver flashes above the lawn, she blinks. The wind vane her father made, the arrowhead impaled in the dirt and the sun and moon quivering in the breeze. The copper pipe that it spun on sticks out sideways.

"What a crazy storm!" Now she doesn't have to take it down at least. She grabs the shaft and with some effort pulls it out of the turf. She props it beside the studio door and goes inside. Bernie studies the painting and can envision a whole series based on these family images. When she completes four or five, she'll call Iraj and see if he would represent her again. She imagines a show at his gallery in the spring, like old times, before the clincher of the twins engulfed everything. Bernie decides she has something good going on with Evelyn in the hollyhocks. She'd stuck with a monochromatic pallet, the olive green of the leaves implied in the grey. She'd painted the holly-hocks in bud not letting them flower, like she imagined her father's mother, thwarted and on hold. The enigma of Evelyn Mary Eddy MacComber.

Bernie picks up the yellowed newspaper clipping from the counter and looks at the twisted wreck of the Model T. "Miss Evelyn Eddy in a dangerous condition following an accident involving the washed-out bridge on range road seven . . . remains unconscious . . . right leg, left collar bone and hip, and four ribs were broken . . . Four other occupants of the car received minor injuries . . . "

To the left of the clipping lie all her childhood and ebullient college photos, and to the right the pictures of Grammy and little Fabian, the wedding pictures of Evelyn and Herbert. Under her wedding dress Evelyn wears the ugly prosthetic shoe to even out her legs. Once Grammy told Bernie that the doctor didn't think she'd make it. How he'd laid her on the kitchen table and only tried to get her straight enough to fit in a coffin.

Bernie sees a tiny print. Fabian, all of six months, sits on a porcelain throne made even higher by a pristine training seat. Gleaming tile surrounds him, his blond hair stands up askew and his plump silky legs stick straight out. With her phone she takes a picture, but before she texts it to David she zooms in on Fabian. Tears glisten on his puffy confused face. Even for 1930's parenting this is amazingly premature potty training. Little Fabian.

"This picture is extraordinary. Freud would be so pleased to have his theory verified!" she writes Peter, and hits send. She looks at the photo of Evelyn on her first day of school. Poor Grammy too, poor Mary Evelyn MacComber.

Two weeks later Bernie studies her kitchen calendar. She unpins it from the wall and flips back to September. The red dot she draws every month is located on September first, Labour Day. The day before the policeman came to tell her about Fabian. Now it's October 15th. She goes to the computer and Googles "reasons for missed period" before she heads out the door to get the kids.

Peter phones while she's driving and the Bluetooth kicks in.

"Where are you?"

"Just going to get the kids, uhm, but something's funny. I'm late. Two weeks."

"How's that possible?"

"Well it's *not* possible. I Googled it though, and it makes sense. Stress can delay a period, and God knows I've been stressed. But I'm going to stop at the drug store just in case."

"I guess so, but I can't imagine. The vasectomy was three years ago. I've probably nailed you every month since then right on your ovulation date."

"Probably."

"So, I can't see how, I mean if they botched the vasectomy this would have happened sooner. Anything on tonight?"

"Piano lessons for Lola, and Eben's going to his friend's house after school. A social studies project I think."

"Okay, see you soon."

∾∾∾

Peeling off her socks in the bathroom Bernie looks at the True-Blue Easy pregnancy test laying on the counter. She opens the box and reads the instructions. A blue line in the second window indicates a positive outcome. Sitting on the toilet she holds the white absorbent tip under the stream of her urine for ten seconds, and watches the capillary action pulling the stain of pee up through the window. She lays it on the counter again and gets into her pajamas and starts brushing her teeth. Glancing down she pushes the toothbrush too far back on her tongue and gags. She leans over the sink, rinses her mouth and looks again. A little blue horizontal line. Bernie stares, picks up the box and rereads the instructions.

"No" she whispers, "please no." She opens the door to the bedroom where Peter lays in bed reading his iPad. "Peter?"

"What's up?"

"Peter. It's positive. I'm pregnant. Fuck! Positive means pregnant right?"

"What? Show me that thing. Where are the instructions? "He scrambles out of bed and goes to the bathroom, reads the box. "Wow! I mean, how do you feel about that?"

"I feel like I'm going to be sick." Bernie turns and loses her dinner in the toilet.

Twenty minutes later Peter sits with his knees drawn up to his chin as he watches Bernie pace at the foot of the bed, tears soaking her face.

"I just can't believe this. Six weeks ago, I was driving home from dropping the kids off for school. The first day of grade one for Moira and Louis, and such sadness and also joy filled me at the same time, you know? But so much satisfaction too. I thought, I've done it, I pulled it off, I did a really good job with them, and now I get my reward. Now I can pursue all the parts of me I had to put in cold storage."

"You *have* done an *amazing* job with them."

"And then that very day, the policeman showed up about my dad! Finally, I thought last week when I gave the key to the realtor, I'm done with that, I'm really done . . . "

"You were *amazingly* tough, through everything."

"And now I can't believe this. Why am I being punished? Why are they telling me I have to choose between killing a baby or killing myself?"

"Well that's a little dramatic. First of all, it's just a tiny ball of cells at this point and . . . "

"I mean the part of me that's been on hold for fourteen years Peter. I just, I can't. I just can't do this!"

"Come, get into bed," says Peter. "You figure out what you need to do, okay? Whatever it is, I'll back you up."

❦❦❦

After dropping the kids off for school, Bernie walks to her studio with a cup of coffee. She pauses at the door and sees the wind vane propped against the wall under the big window. She opens the door and steps inside, stares at her paint brushes standing on end in the Mason jar by the sink. In a moment she turns and goes outside and looks at the wind vane. It winks in the sun. She steps inside again, sits on her stool and looks at Evelyn.

She thinks about her dream. The bell tolling. Her bags were packed, but by someone else. A warning. The bell. It tolls for me, and that dark-haired man so determined and oddly familiar, just the feel of him. Evelyn watches her from behind the shade of her hat, and Bernie suddenly knows. That would be enough time for him to reincarnate wouldn't it? It's him, her father. He's come home to roost.

❦❦❦

Peter walks to his office door and looks through the glass partition. He watches the guys in the tech department, everyone busy making changes for the Terminal D construction drawings. He has an hour before the engineers show up for the consultant meeting. He locks his door and goes back to the desk, sits in his big black rolling chair. Has he got the number on his cell phone? Yes, that's a relief. Usually Bernie's the one who phones David but here is the contact. He presses the mobile number and waits.

"Peter?" David's surprised voice.

"Hi David, yeah, it's me. Look, I'm really sorry to phone you at work. Have you got a minute?"

"What's up? Is Bernie all right?"

"Well that's just it."

"What do you mean?"

"Bernie's fine don't worry. It's just a weird development that's occurred. We just found out she's pregnant."

"Seriously! She'll be forty-five! Well I don't know what to say. Is that good news?"

"No, it's not. She doesn't want to do it. She says she's done. I can totally understand that. Bernie thought the next chapter of her life was about to open up. She's done a fabulous job with the four of them. But what worries me is this crazy idea she's come up with."

"Mmm?"

"She's convinced herself that the baby is Fabian. She thinks because of a dream, and some notion of Hindu timelines for reincarnation. Oh yes, and something about her father's wind vane falling off the roof, she thinks she's pregnant with her late father."

"Wow!"

"Fucking hippie ancestry, I guess. You don't seem to fall prey to that. But I'm just worried for her. Should I go along with this? Bernie's so maternal, I'm just worried she might regret it later on."

"Do *you* want another baby?"

"Hell no. The twins are finally old enough to actually do stuff, ski and hike. No more diapers. But this is just such bizarre thinking on her part. She's convinced that somehow Fabian's pulled a fast one. That he 'reversed' my vasectomy and has weaseled his way in. It's crazy."

"Hmm. I don't know. All I can say is it must be hard being female. I guess I'd say go along with this, humour her. It's a form of denial, but maybe it's protective."

"All right. You think so?"

"Yeah. Like you say, for someone like Bernie it's a tough decision."

"Thanks man, that helps."

"No problem. Phone again if you need to. I hope she'll be all right."

⊷⊶⊷

Bernie waits with the other mothers and fathers outside the red door. She tries to avoid eye contact. Annette will want to pin her down about volunteering for classroom rep. The position hasn't been filled yet. She listens to Lisa and Rick discuss the logistics of hockey practice. All these normal parents, with their normal, healthy lives, and here she stands, pregnant. Oddly enough, pregnant with the reincarnation of her late father Fabian McComber. The procedure is booked for Friday. The bell rings and the kids stream out. She gathers them up before their friends can distract them.

"Sorry guys, we've got to run. Umm, a delivery is showing up soon, so I have to get home."

In the van their voices immerse her. If she focuses, she can forget everything but the logistics of Moira and Louis' playground politics, Lola's next science project. She imbeds herself in that world.

"After dinner, who wants to go to Michael's? Lola needs plasticine and poster board for her diorama."

"Yay!" they all shout. They stop at the grocery store on the way home for whipping cream and berries. Lola has been watching Nigella Lawson YouTube videos, and the idea of trifle consumes her.

Walking in the front door she sees Eben's size twelve high tops.

"Eben?" she shouts. No answer, so she starts to climb the stairs. Bernie knocks on the door, waits a moment, and then opens it. He sits on the side of the bed his elbows on his knees and his head hanging. He looks up, surprised to see her. He takes in her face.

"Hi, bud. How was your day?"

"Uh, okay."

"Are you sure, you seem kind of worried." He looks back at her, studies the black circles under her eyes. The familiar haggard expression.

"No, I'm fine."

"You're not still feeling guilty about the hedgehog, are you? Remember I'm the one who dropped the ball on that one. *I'm* the mother. You can't be expected to know everything, and besides Cynthia survived. It all worked out."

"No, it's not that, I mean, I'm fine. I just have a lot of homework."

"Okay . . . You sure? Chicken fricassee for dinner tonight." Bernie goes out and shuts the door.

On Friday Bernie drops the kids at school and then takes Angus to the dog park. Peter will meet her at the house at ten and drive her to the clinic. The day is clear and beautiful. Fifteen degrees already and by afternoon it will feel like summer. She opens the door and Angus squeezes out behind her back, leaps over the low wire dividing the park from the road, and starts zigzagging through the long grass in search of mice. She turns east to do her habitual loop through the poplars and then down along the river, grateful the park looks deserted this morning.

In her head she talks to him. Tells him what he needs to know before he goes. First of all, she says, *ask* before you impose yourself on a woman. She must want you, and you're a handful, so pick a mind-blowingly maternal woman, okay? You understand it's not just about you? That's a twenty-year commitment you're asking of her, no, it's a life sentence, and she has to want you desperately.

Also, don't do drugs. That didn't work out so well, did it? There are no shortcuts. You have to feel the pain, just feel it and then it goes away. Don't be scared, everyone has some, and if you experience it, if you let it run through you like water, eventually you'll be rinsed clean. You have to be patient and stick with the feeling. I know it's uncomfortable.

Fabian listens, floating quietly inside the potent brew of Bernie gearing herself up. A life skills recap. Handling women 101. She's right of course, and because he feels bad about her distress, he makes an effort to concentrate.

Also, next lifetime, remember there is a line dividing children and parents. You can't cross that line. You take

183

care of them; *they don't take care of you*. Pick a good enough mother this time, one that can really fill you up. Then you won't be jealous of your kids when they come along, and if you are a good enough father maybe they'll even visit you when you're old. Actually, even if you get a rotten mother next time, be the parent you wished you'd had. It feels better that way; you'll be proud of yourself, and the kids will definitely thank you.

Yes, yes, I know. Bune and I went through all of that. Stop rubbing it in. I know how I failed you.

About women: Look beyond the whole idea of beauty and sex. Remember there is a person under that skin. Love the person, see what she feels, what she thinks, if you do that . . .

Fabian curls his blastosphere self into an even tighter ball and wishes he could roll under something to muffle the noise. *Okay, okay,* he shouts. Please just stop talking. Stop talking and I'll be good.

Peter and Bernie sit in the parking lot.

"Are you okay?"

Bernie exhales. Looks at the stucco wall of the clinic.

"It's funny. When I found out I was pregnant with all the babies, even though we hadn't planned Eben, even when I found out the twins were going to be twins, I felt so happy. I clutched them to my heart. But this time everything just screams 'no'. This is not my baby, and I cannot keep him. He would be a cuckoo in the nest. He'd hurt our kids."

Peter looks down at his feet on the rubber mat. He takes her hand and holds it.

184

"You ready then?"

"Yes, I am."

"Well let's go."

☙◦☙

Bernie lies back on the inclined surgical table under the sheet. The nurse, her name tag says Nancy, clips the heart-rate monitor to her finger.

"How are you feeling? Pretty woozy?"

"Like I've had three glasses of wine, but not sick."

"Lorazepam's good stuff. Now I'm just going to insert this injection port into your vein and tape it on. That's what we'll use for the conscious sedation; I'll hook you up in a minute. When you're feeling really happy the doctor will come in and after ten minutes it will all be over."

Bernie looks around the surgical suite. It's so odd, she seems to speak without slurring, but whole sections of the room disappear into black holes in her vision. She looks over at the nurse, a grandmotherly woman in flower print scrubs. She makes her eyes focus. Tulips.

"Could you tell me something before you go?" asks Bernie.

"Sure."

Later standing over the autoclave in the hallway, Nancy lays out the speculum and dilators on the wire racks.

Lauren comes up behind her, putting on her coat.

"Do you want a coffee? I'm going to Tim Horton's."

"Sure. Just cream please." She closes the hatch and pushes the power button. "Do you ever wonder, I mean . . . That last patient, I don't know."

"Bernadette MacComber?"

"Yeah. Nice woman. She asked me before I knocked her out to look up the birth date of the baby if she'd have kept it. Not that I haven't been asked that before."

"Mmmhmm, me too."

"Well I looked it up on the wheel and told her. April eleventh I think, and the weird thing is she *laughed*. She said, 'that's my father's birthday!' and she threw back her head and laughed. It seemed so callous somehow, she didn't seem the type."

"Just the drugs talking, I think. Lorazepam can do funny things. You want a muffin too?"

"Yes thanks."

⊷⊷⊷

For six nights now, Bernie hasn't slept. This morning she calls the counsellor she saw at the clinic.

"Hi Judith. This is Bernadette MacComber, I talked to you last week."

"I remember. How are you?"

"Fine I think. The bleeding's stopped, but the problem is I can't sleep. I get two hours a night max. I'm feeling a bit desperate. I looked on the internet . . . "

"Oh, *don't do that*! Stay off the internet. You can get all sorts of misinformation. Sleeplessness is a common post-procedure symptom. Your hormones are all out of whack. What day is it?"

"Six, I think."

"You're almost there. Hold on. In a few more days you'll be back to normal."

"That's all it is?"

"Yes, I promise."

"That's a relief. Thank you."

"No worries. Call any time."

Bernie slips her phone back into her vest pocket and downs the last of her cold coffee. She turns to her painting, the sun streams in the studio window. The big canvas she stretched to the frame yesterday measures four-feet square. She had roughed out the shapes already, very simple in this case, just one massive sphere hurtling through space. A cannonball of intention. She squeezes out some raw umber and alizarin red on her pallet, adds some black, then dumps her water jar at the sink and fills it again. She returns to the painting and starts shading. She works the sphere up, making the planet more and more three-dimensional. So round, it looks ready to blow through the canvas.

This time Fabian goes through the arrivals gate. He stands on the whispering conveyor belt with big eyes, but the white walls slipping past him offer nothing in way of explanation. Finally, he stops before the frosted doors. They slide open with a hiss. The conveyor belt delivers him, and the doors shut behind. Fabian starts to shake. A grey and smoky place. A horde of beings stand, all watching him. Silent *throngs* of them. Some have wings; some tails and funny heads like gorgons. A few look distinctly furry but with human faces. Others make quick flights around him like birds, but then settle back into the crowd whispering. Fabian presses his lips together, so he won't cry; he looks behind him but can't see the doors anymore. The feather mangled and crushed in the palm of his hand is all he has to hold onto.

Nothing happens. None of the beings approach him. What are they waiting for? They just stand patiently and watch. Finally, a murmur begins somewhere at the back. It ripples and grows in volume. He can make out words now.

"He's coming! The Maestro! Genius! The Great Trickster!"

The words rise to a crescendo of bird-like squawking and growls, and just when Fabian thinks he can't possibly stand anymore, the crowd parts. Fabian squints down the aisle as the beings all pull back. And he sees him. Like thunder he comes striding, the cloud gown billowing behind him. His legs a churning wave, his face an island of certainty. Fabian ducks his head and starts to run. He runs, and runs, until at last he hits him. So solid. So warm.

"There you are!" Bune picks up Fabian and hoists him to his shoulder. The crowd erupts in a roar and Fabian hides his face against the angel's hair. "We'll go in a moment." Bune turns toward the crowd and Fabian feels him waving. "Maestro! Magician!" they chant. As he walks the roar diminishes and suddenly, as if they have passed through more doors, all is quiet. Fabian lifts his face and looks around. They stand in a meadow of long windswept grass. Above them a blue and sunny sky. Bune sets him on his feet.

"Where are we?"

"Corridor *Eight!*" Bune unfolds his wings, flexes them fully and smiles down at Fabian. "Much better for flying!" He holds Fabian out at arm's length. "Let's have a look at you. You've grown! You look about six now, and you're much more proportionate."

Fabian pats himself down. Head not so big, little boy testicles.

"Hey! They reduced my equipment!"

"Do you mind? How does you new body feel compared to the old one?"

Fabian grips his little package, tilts his head from side to side, considering. He breathes a big sigh.

"Actually, the old equipment weighed me down."

"Excellent, our work on Corridor Nine must have registered. In your last assignment you achieved some balance."

"Assignment? You mean lifetime? How can you call that a lifetime? I never got bigger than a lima bean!"

"Ah yes, but finally you completed an assignment that you didn't end by your own hand, and thus here we are, on Corridor Eight!" Fabian stares at the fragrant rustling grasses surrounding them, bending to the wind like waves. "By the way, could I have my feather back?" The towhead boy looks up slowly, extends his hand and opens it. He grins. Bune takes the mangled, sweaty scrap. "Thank you."

"All those creatures back there. They were chanting "Maestro, Magician . . . ""

"Let's just say, Fabian MacComber has become something of legend. All bets were out, if I would succeed or fail," Bune's calloused face wrinkles into a smile. He looks into Fabian's eyes. The two other heads pop out of his shoulders. "Take your pick. Eeny meany miney mo."

"The dog please," says Fabian, and soon he sinks his fingers into the thick ruff of fur.

"And now we'll walk."

ᴑᴖᴑᴖᴑ

Eben stands at his bedroom window and looks at the first wet flakes of winter falling lazy in the dark. Through the snow the light still burns in his mother's studio. He checks the time on his phone, then goes down the stairs to the kitchen, and boils the kettle.

Bernie finishes the surrounding space, working the paint into the canvas, sweeping and grinding it into weather systems. The planet floats, bobs buoyantly. Now she will start laying down the biosphere. It needs to be completely forested and she decides on deciduous trees. Poplars. She jumps. The door opens and snow blows in.

Eben stands barefoot in his boxer shorts and a hoody, two mugs steam in his hands.

"What are you doing? You'll freeze!"

"I couldn't sleep."

"Well then, we're good company." His hands are full, so Bernie walks over and shuts the door. Then she goes to the back wall and unearths a folding chaise lounge and drags it close to the Franklin stove. She grabs a sleeping bag and pulls it out of its stuff sack. His full-grown man feet are wet and red with cold. Surprisingly he sits and lets her dry them with a clean rag, then takes the sleeping bag from her, crawls in and pulls it up to his armpits. When he's reclining on the chaise, she hands him his tea.

"Why couldn't you sleep?" Silence. Bernie turns and goes back to putting in the trees. Soon the grayish groves of bare branches radiate out into space.

"It's a very small planet."

"Yes."

190

"What will you call this one?"

"Whole."

"Hole? I wouldn't call it 'Hole'. It's the opposite."

"No, 'Whole.' Complete, intact, healed, all of a piece."

"Oh, that makes sense. What season will you choose?"

"Mmm, I'm thinking fall. I'll start putting in the leaves soon." She stands back and squints, returns to her work. "What time is it?"

"Twelve thirty."

"Why couldn't you sleep?"

Silence.

"Do you ever wonder, Mom, what's better. I mean, have you ever been in a situation where you have to choose between everyone hating you, or you hating yourself?"

"Oh yes. That's happened all my life. And which did you pick?"

"The lonely choice."

"Not as lonely as the alternative. Who hates you?"

"Every girl in the school." Bernie studies him for a minute, goes back to painting.

"It started when Madison Harding got into Jake's Gmail . . . "

"What?"

"They were working on a group project, and he didn't sign out of his Gmail when he went to talk to someone. She thought she was being funny, and she sent this stupid email to everyone on his contact list."

"Good Lord! That's terrible! What did she write?"

"Oh, something like; 'I'm gay and like to wear women's lingerie,' I forget all the details, but really dumb. The problem was the email went to this guy who interviewed him for a job at Sport Chek. The guy must think he's an idiot. Jake thinks he won't get the job now."

Bernie opens a tube of cadmium yellow and squeezes it onto her palette.

"So where do you come in? I don't understand?" She mixes the yellow with a little umber, some white.

"I'm Jake's best friend. Madison thinks I should talk to him. He says he's going to tell the principal if he doesn't get the job. I don't blame him, but Madison told her friends, told Leanne. They're all saying we're being too hard on her, that we'll ruin her life, it was just a joke . . . "

She starts applying the leaves, some golden, some darker. Some white as if turning in the wind.

"Aren't you going to put any leaves on the ground?"

"Nah, I figure they can just blow out into space."

"That won't work. If there's no atmosphere on this planet, how can there be a water cycle? There'd be no way to support plant growth."

"Hmm, I guess you're right. I'll leaf up the forest floor a bit." She turns to reload her brush, "and I think this mess should stay between Madison and Jake. It has nothing to do with you. You were right not to get involved, and Jake's your best friend. Who is this Leanne?"

"A girl."

"Well, you made the right choice. You have to trust your gut. They'll come around eventually. At least the good ones will." Outside the big, wet flakes fall soft on the lawn. They land and melt away until the ground gets cold enough, and then they begin to pile up.

"I didn't want to tell you this."

"Tell me what?"

"I bombed my chemistry test."

Outside the snow keeps falling with increasing certainty. The white starts to blanket every hump in the grass, a herd of Moira's plastic cows in the sandbox, Angus's gnawed bone, an elastic-band ball forgotten by Louis. Eben talks and Bernie listens. She works, and he talks into the new day.

⊖⊖⊖

At seven, Peter wakes. He listens to the silence and wonders at the different quality of light, looks out the window and surveys the first snowfall. Rolling over he sees Bernie's vacant pillow. Putting on his bathrobe he walks to the kitchen to find her. Maybe she's in the laundry room? No. He checks the kids' bedrooms and finds Eben missing too. But her van still sits parked in the garage. He pulls on his boots and steps out the back door. A thread of smoke rises out of the studio chimney as the sky turns to pink. He walks, each step revealing a green footprint in the snow, until he reaches the studio.

Peter turns the handle, pushes the door open, and then he stops. In the small room Eben stretches out in a sleeping bag on a chaise lounge in front of the Franklin stove. His arm dangles to the floor and the auburn hair covers his face. Across from him Bernie curls on another chaise lounge under two winter coats. She drools on the fleece jacket wadded under her head for a pillow. Peter steps in quietly and pulls the door closed. The sunrise bounces off the snow, and the white radiance illuminates the planet on the easel.

Later in the winter, guests at a dinner party will gather and try to name it. It would make a great ecological logo says one friend. Someone else compares it to a seed pod

193

about to burst. Another thinks of Lola's hedgehog, curled tight. But a fourth says, no. This is the microscopic view of an ovum at the moment of fertilization, the sperm cells radiating, fighting to be the first to grind their pointy-heads through the tough outer membrane, to hit the mark and set off that genetic chain reaction.

For awhile Peter stands and studies the painting. He watches Bernie and Eben breathing, and then he steps back outside and softly closes the door. It's Saturday. He'll let them sleep as long as they need to.

ACKNOWLEDGEMENTS

The great E.B. White once said, "I admire anyone who has the guts to write anything at all." Writing a book is a frightening business, and it takes a village at your back to keep pen to paper. Thank you to my sister, Ruey Stocking, and my many good friends, for their feedback and encouragement along the way. In particular, thank you to Monica Skrukwa, for her unwavering conviction that I could do this. At many points I would have quit but for her insistence.

To my mother and father, Laurel Ellison and John Stocking, for a childhood rich in experience. For the art and literature, exposure to many cultures, the nature, food, and pets. I now realize a childhood of this calibre is rare. Thank you to my lovely mother-in-law, Joan Reinhardt, who liked me from the start, and who always shows up when the going gets rough. To my Aunt Liane, writer, professor, and inspiration, thank you for your thoughtful reading of the early draft.

Thanks to Thistledown Press. I am grateful indeed to land in the capable hands of this venerable Canadian publisher. Thanks as well to my excellent editor Harriet Richards.

I wrote this book in English 598 at the University of Calgary, and arrived, a somewhat shell-shocked recovering housewife who'd lost access to her words. Providentially, the class taught by Aritha van Herk remyelinated my verbal brain, and probably made me think harder than I've ever thought before. Thank you Aritha, for your generous encouragement, and the rigour and dedication of your teaching. I was lucky indeed to walk into your classroom.

Thank you to Lori Hahnel, who on multiple occasions reduced my stress exponentially with her generous advice. I am but one example of her magnanimous fostering of Calgary writers. The prodigious creative hub, Alexandra Writer's Centre, in particular classes under Robin van Eck, built my courage and fortified my portfolio. Thank you.

To my children Avery, Nathan, and Josephine, thank you for your patience with the wild ups and downs of my creative process, and your grounded, often spot on literary feedback. Thank you, Josephine, as well, for insisting I submit my painting as cover art, and for devising the title! Watching you three go forward is my greatest pride and delight.

Finally, to Paul, for putting beans on the table, keeping the roof over our heads, and all of us under it dancing. Thank you for really hearing my stories. You are my home and foundation.

Burdened by the notion that a career should encompass everything, Sophie Stocking changed her major so often she narrowly escaped a degree in General Studies. Chapters in social work, architecture, and motherhood followed. She finally noticed that she'd always been writing, and in terms of encompassing everything, stories fit the bill. Sophie found the courage to pursue fiction at the Alexandra Writer's Centre, and went on to study under Aritha van Herk at the University of Calgary. *Corridor Nine* is her debut novel. She hopes one day, to own a hedgehog.